M000296707

LOVE ME

MARCIA LYNN McCLURE

Published by Distractions Ink
P.O. Box 15971
Rio Rancho, NM 87174

©Copyright 2006, 2008, 2012 by M. L. Meyers
A.K.A. Marcia Lynn McClure
Cover Photography by
©Tomas del Amo | Dreamstime.com
Cover Design by
Sheri L. Brady | MightyPhoenixDesignStudio.com

Second Printed Edition: 2012

McClure, Marcia Lynn, 1965—
Love Me: a novella/by Marcia Lynn McClure.

ISBN: 978-0-9852807-2-7

Library of Congress Control Number: 2012934962

Printed in the United States of America

To First Love…
The one we all experienced,
The one we learned from,
The one we never completely get over.

PART ONE

CHAPTER ONE

"Jacey? Would you turn on the pumpkin patch sprinklers on your way out, please?" Mandy Whittaker asked.

Jacey rolled her eyes. Exhaling an irritated sigh, she said, "Yes, Mother." Slipping on her shoes, Jacey picked up her backpack and headed out the kitchen door.

"And do it with the right attitude," her mother called after her. "If you want to make any money off those pumpkins, you better take care of them."

"I know, I know," Jacey mumbled, twisting the outside faucet handle. She smiled as she watched the sprinklers sputter and bloom. If her last count of the pumpkins were correct, at three bucks a pop, she'd have a good one hundred and fifty dollars to her name by the time Halloween was over.

Pumpkins—one of Jacey's favorite things in all the world! She loved to watch the small pumpkin sprouts break through the rich, dark soil in spring. Once the vines began running willy-nilly in the patch, she relished carefully wandering in their midst, searching for the bright yellow-orange blossoms—the promise of the rich orange treasure to come at harvesttime. The anticipation of earning a wad of cash from their sale was sheer bonus, for in the end it was all about the joy of the patch and the harvest—whether or not she whined to her mother about tending it.

Homecoming was scheduled two weeks after Halloween. Jacey was hoping the money from the pumpkin sales would be enough to buy a dress—just in case someone asked her to go. She knew chances were slim to none anybody would ask *her*, a lowly sophomore. Still, she had her secret dreams. Therefore, just in case a miracle did occur, Jacey wanted to be certain she had the means to purchase the white sequin-drenched formal she'd seen at the mall.

Jacey gazed up into the clear blue of an early October sky and sighed with contentment. Closing her eyes, she inhaled deeply the warm scent of burning leaves, reveling in the feel of the cool breeze kissing her cheeks.

"Come on, Jacey!" Scott called. Jacey opened her eyes to see him running out the back door of the house next to hers. "You'll make us late!"

As usual, the very sight of Scott caused her heart to leap wildly in her chest.

"Me?" she giggled. "What're you talking about? I've been ready for hours!"

"Yeah, right," he said, shoving a final bite of toast into his mouth and pulling his football jersey on over his head. He opened the driver's side door of the old beat-up red pickup he called "Cherry" and tossed in his backpack. "Come on, sugar-britches," he said, rushing to the passenger's side of the pickup and opening the door for Jacey.

Jacey paused for a moment, still mesmerized by the mere sight of him. Scott Pendleton—brown hair, blue eyes, and gorgeous! Far beyond cute, Scott was absolutely thoroughly handsome—the handsomest boy at Ridge High School! At eighteen, Scott was not only handsome, polite, funny, and totally buff, he was also the school's hotshot running back! In every way, Scott was the very embodiment of any teenage girl's dream.

As with every moment Jacey was in Scott's presence, she silently wished she were older—eighteen instead of just sixteen. She wished she were prettier—a better match for the best catch at Ridge. Her smile faded a moment as she suddenly became desperately aware of herself—desperately aware of her unworthiness to even dream of such a boy. Yet dream of him she did, just like every other girl at their school.

"Come on, Pumpkin Patch Patty," Scott said, taking Jacey's backpack and tossing it in the pickup next to his. "I can't get another tardy this week, or Coach will have my head."

"Sorry," Jacey said, smiling at him as she climbed into the pickup. Scott returned her smile and closed the door. He hurried to the driver's side and climbed in himself.

"Let's go," he said, smiling at her. He turned the key in the ignition, and the truck rumbled to life—as did the pickup's sound system speakers. Jacey smiled as John Cougar Mellencamp's gravel voice rocked "Jack and Diane." One of the many things Scott and Jacey held in common was their love for vintage music. There were things they disagreed on—Scott swore the 1980s saw the best music ever recorded, and Jacey insisted Elvis Presley and Donny Osmond were the best singers ever born.

With a smile and another wink, he threw the pickup into first, holding the clutch to smoke some rubber. He popped the clutch, however, when Mrs. Pendleton appeared at the Pendletons' front door wagging an index finger at her son.

Rolling down her window, Jacey called, "'Bye, Mrs. Pendleton!" Scott's mother smiled and waved as Scott shifted the pickup into second.

"You coming to the game tonight, Jace?" Scott asked as they drove.

"Don't I always come to your games?" Jacey answered, smiling at her handsome friend. Scott smiled in return, laid his right arm along the back of the seat, and affectionately squeezed Jacey's shoulder. As always, his touch caused Jacey's breath to catch, her skin to tingle. "In fact," Jacey began, placing a pensive index finger to her chin as she looked at him, "I can't remember a time before I was always coming to your games."

"Liar," he said, smiling. "I didn't start football 'til junior high."

"I know," Jacey giggled—though she remembered

very well the day sports had replaced her as Scott Pendleton's favorite pastime.

Growing up next door to each other, Jacey couldn't remember a time when Scott wasn't a part of her everyday life. As children, they'd run through the sprinklers, ridden bikes, played with matches, and just about every other thing they could think of. Fast and best friends, Scott and Jacey had been nearly inseparable—until the day Scott started junior high, leaving Jacey still in elementary school. Yet although Scott left early childhood behind, he never quit being Jacey's best friend. Most of the free time he did have, especially in summers, he spent with Jacey. At least until Scott entered the eighth grade and discovered that not only did his guy friends offer the lure of mischief and masculine adventure but girls had gotten a lot more interesting too. And therein began the misery of Jacey's own life.

Jacey Whittaker had loved Scott Pendleton for as long as she could remember. Loved him first as a friend and then as a heroine loved a hero. And then—then along about the time Scott discovered other girls— Jacey had begun to love him as the boy of her dreams. For five long years, Jacey secreted the type of feelings she held for Scott—as well as the depth of them. Furthermore, as Scott had begun to mature, to grow more handsome, charming, and charismatic, other girls had begun to notice him too.

Before Jacey had entered Ridge High School as a freshman, she had been fairly unaware of Scott's magnetism where girls were concerned. After all, it had been four years since she had attended the same school as Scott. Yet on her first day of school at Taylor Ridge, Jacey had become painfully aware of his popularity among those of the female gender. As she'd watched the gaggle of girls following her dream boy around—as she watched the way the girls giggled and whispered whenever he walked by and especially as she saw the hateful looks directed at her when she was with Scott— Jacey knew Scott Pendleton belonged to the world. In those early teen years, Scott moved beyond the little girl next door and into the world of flirtatious young women.

Certainly Scott never let on anything had changed. He still came over to Jacey's house to hang out, still asked her to do stuff with him, still drove her to school every morning. What was different was Jacey. Her feelings had changed, and Scott seemed none the wiser. Jacey wanted it that way. Actually, what she wanted was for Scott to feel the same way about her that she did him, but she knew such a dream was impossible. The hardest part of it all was watching Scott date other girls. He'd never had a serious or steady girlfriend, but Jacey knew one day he would, and she dreaded it, had nightmares about it, and cried a river of tears in anticipation of it. Still, what was to be done except endure? More than once the thought of confessing her feelings for him had run through her mind, but Jacey had quickly squelched it, determining it was better to have Scott as a friend than not at all.

Yet it remained difficult, watching him with other girls. Watching him drive off with one in his pickup on warm summer evenings, knowing he was with another girl. Each time he left for a date, Jacey's mind was on fire with jealousy, disappointment, and heartache. Still, she never let him know it. She wanted Scott to be happy, to enjoy his life. She just wished she were the part of his life making him happy.

"Look," Scott said, jerking Jacey's thoughts back to the moment at hand. "I brought this for you. It's spirit day, you know."

"What?" Jacey asked as Scott began rummaging around in his backpack with one hand.

"Well," he said, still rummaging, "I know you don't think you look good in maroon and gold…but you've gotta wear the school colors on game day, Jace," he said. Awkwardly, he pulled a maroon-and-gold football jersey out of his backpack and handed it to Jacey. "There you go. Throw that on over your clothes," he said.

"Your jersey?" Jacey asked as she stared at the jersey in her hands. Her heart began to hammer madly at the thought of wearing Scott's jersey.

"It's an old one," he said, smiling at her. "There's a little tear at the bottom somewhere…but I figure you can tuck it in."

Jacey held the jersey up, staring in disbelief at the gold number sixteen printed on the maroon base.

"You can have it," Scott said. "Mom made me clean out my closet, and I figured you could use it on spirit days and then for whatever else after that." Jacey glanced at him, hoping he didn't notice the way her hands trembled as she held the jersey. "Go ahead!" he laughed. "Throw it on! Let's see what a sexy angel you are wearing my football jersey." He smiled at her and winked, and she glared at him.

"You're never going to let me forget that, are you?" Jacey asked. Scott knew full well to what she was referring. After all, he'd teased her about it forever—ever since, at the age of nine, Jacey had snuck into the very back of her mother's closet and absconded her mother's pretty "angel dress," donning it as her angel costume in the Christmas pageant program at church. The angel dress had proved to be quite the talk of the congregation, as well as proving to humiliate Jacey's mother nearly beyond recovery. The white gossamer negligee that hung in the back of her mother's closet had seemed so beautiful to Jacey's innocent and naive eyes. Long, flowing, white chiffon with white feathers at the sleeves and hem—the perfect angel costume. Yet Jacey had sensed enough about the angel dress being special that she hadn't asked her mother's permission to borrow it. She'd simply hidden it in her little duffle bag and snuck it to the church. When the time came for Jacey to make her appearance in the pageant, she stepped onto the stage donning the beautiful angel dress and causing a ripple of laughter to wash over the audience.

"I don't think anyone *should* forget that, Jace," Scott chuckled.

Jacey blushed at the memory of her mother

explaining that the gossamer gown was not an angel dress but rather a nightgown Jacey's father had given her on their anniversary. Scott, being two years older than Jacey, was already a little wiser to the ways of the world and had dubbed Jacey "sexy angel" because of her loveable innocence in the matter. Still, Jacey loved the pet name. Of all the pet names Scott had bestowed upon her over the years, "sexy angel" was her favorite—even if it did border on questionable when heard out of context.

"Throw the jersey on, Jace," Scott said. "Show some school spirit!"

Jacey giggled and shook her head. Scott was a die-hard school spirit advocate. She guessed seeing everyone wearing the school colors helped to buoy up his confidence before a game. In reality, for the fabulous player he was, Scott struggled with self-confidence. For the beautiful, adorable, funny boy he was, Scott struggled with self-esteem. Perhaps it was the rocky marriage his parents displayed, or perhaps it was just a streak of humility or lack of typical teenage ego, but whatever the reason, Scott was a humble boy, and the fact only served to enhance his charm.

"Maroon washes me out," Jacey told him as she obeyed and slipped the jersey over her head.

"Nothing washes you out, Jace," he told her.

"Oh my heck! It's huge!" she exclaimed as she awkwardly struggled in the pickup to pull the jersey on completely. "Almost to my knees!"

"Maybe you should lose the jeans and wear it as a dress," Scott chuckled. He smiled at her as he studied her for a moment. "It's perfect! I like it," he said with a wink. "Just for one day, right?" Jacey smiled and shook her head, amused at his insistence.

"You are too into this, Scottie," she told him. "I look like an idiot."

"You look adorable," he told her, smiling. "There'll be lots of girls wearing jerseys today. It's spirit—"

"Spirit day. I know," Jacey interrupted with a giggle. Jacey smoothed the jersey over her lap, momentarily blissful as the scent of Scott's cologne filled her lungs. "Um…when's the last time you washed this, babe?" she asked. Her skin was alive, tingling with goose bumps at the thought of wearing something that had once been worn against Scott's body.

"I don't know," Scott said, shrugging his shoulders. "I know I didn't wear it in a game though. We got our new jerseys, and I just hung that one in the closet."

"And…and I've always wondered," Jacey began, "why sixteen? Did they just assign you guys your numbers? Or did you choose it?"

"I've been wearing sixteen for four years, Jace," Scott said. "You just now noticed?"

Jacey shrugged and said, "Oh, I knew your number was sixteen, dummy. I just…I just never thought to ask if there's a reason."

"There's a reason," Scott said.

Jacey frowned when he neglected to explain the reason to her, however.

"What's the reason?" she asked.

"It's a secret," he whispered. "I could tell you…but then I'd have to kill you."

Jacey rolled her eyes, smiling at his completely predictable, completely cliché response.

"You're a brat," she told him, blushing with pride as they drove into the school parking lot. She didn't even mind the hateful look some girls gave her as they drove past. Being with Scott was worth all the hateful looks in the world. "Come on, Scottie," she said as he turned the pickup into a parking space. "Just tell me. Why did you choose sixteen as your number?"

Scott put the shift in first and turned off the ignition. Smiling, he turned to her and said, "Figure it out. Sixteen candles, sweet sixteen…"

"Sweet sixteen and never been kissed!" Jacey exclaimed, her eyes widening. "You were sixteen before you ever kissed anyone?"

"Ppfff!" Scott exclaimed, frowning and feigning offense. "Be serious. I chose the number when I was a freshman…long before I was sixteen." Jacey smiled and wrinkled her nose at him even though her heart had began to ache over the knowledge Scott had kissed other girls. Oh, he'd never really told her he had…but she knew. She knew. "I will tell you this, sexy jersey girl," he continued, "you're somewhat on the right track to guessing."

"And so," Jacey said, sighing, "Scott Pendleton remains a mystery."

Scott chuckled and opened his door, stepping out

11

of his truck and into the world of Ridge High School popularity—into Ridge High School's parking lot and away from Jacey.

"You betcha," he said, smiling. He hurried around the pickup and opened Jacey's door for her. As she climbed down, he said, "I gotta run. I gotta talk to Coach before class. You gotta ride home for today?" he asked, reaching past Jacey to retrieve his backpack from the seat.

"Yeah. Kerry said she'd take me home," Jacey answered.

"If you'd let me teach you to drive a stick...you could take the truck home and just bring it back to me when you come for the game," he said.

"I know, I know," Jacey said. Scott had been trying to talk her into letting him teach her to drive his truck ever since she'd gotten her driver's license two months before.

"This weekend, Jace," he said firmly. "You're learning this weekend."

Jacey smiled, delighted at the prospect of spending time with him. "Okay. Okay. I'll do it."

"Good deal," he said, smiling down at her. He ran a hand over her shoulder and down her arm, sending goose bumps traveling down her arm following the route of his touch. "Have a good day. All right?" he said as he turned to leave.

"You too," she said.

Scott looked back at her, smiled, and waved as Liz Robertson hurried over to him. Jacey waved back at him, her smile fading, however, as she watched Liz take hold of Scott's arm. She watched as Scott laughed at something Liz said. Her ears felt hot and her stomach churned with miserable jealousy. She knew Liz had asked Scott out, that he had said yes, and that they had plans together for the next evening. It's why Jacey had accepted Chris Santore's offer to take her out the same night. Knowing she had to try and let go of her dreams of owning Scott, Jacey had decided to begin dating herself. Up until then, she hadn't. Not caring a whit for any other boy, save Scott, Jacey had done little one-on-one socializing with other boys, but the reality was fast falling over her Scott would someday find someone to love. Jacey knew if she didn't try to find someone to love second best…she'd be miserable forever over not having Scott.

Still, having to endure watching other girls smile with, flirt with, and go on dates with Scott only continued to become more difficult to deal with. Not easier.

She watched Scott walk toward the gym for a moment longer before turning and heading to her own class. Yet as she walked, she allowed pride to lift her spirits a bit. Pride in the looks the other girls gave her as she passed them wearing Scott's old jersey. By now everyone in the school knew Scott and Jacey were just neighbors, friends of convenience. But Jacey knew there was always just a bit of doubt in their minds. Especially on days like this—days when Jacey was able to display some sort of connection with Scott other girls couldn't.

As some girls glared at Jacey, others smiled and giggled, giving her a thumbs-up, delighted and showing their support of Jacey's one-upping the snotty girls who all thought they were good enough to snag Scott Pendleton. Yet throughout the day, Jacey felt melancholy, blue, and rather lonely. Perhaps it was the faint scent of Scott's all too familiar cologne filling her senses. Perhaps it was the constant reminder on a game day that Scott was a senior, close to graduation, close to leaving for college, close to leaving Jacey heartbroken and alone.

Even the yearbook staff taking pictures of Scott and Jacey in their matching jerseys at lunch did little to lift her spirits—for Jacey was beginning to worriedly anticipate losing Scott. Not that she'd ever owned him—not since he'd started junior high and discovered guy friends and girls, anyway. But his leaving was inevitable. Jacey had helped Scott decide on which colleges to apply to. Scott would leave. He would, and Jacey knew she would never recover.

♥

Scott watched Jacey enter the stadium. He smiled, pleased at the way his old football jersey completely enveloped her. He shook his head, amazed she could possibly think she didn't look good in maroon. Jacey Whittaker looked good in anything! His eyes narrowed as he studied her for a moment, the perfect curve of her smile, the youthful flash in her hazel eyes, the way the softness of her brown, highlighted hair moved as she turned her head. The football jersey hid the perfect,

14

very womanly shape of her figure—the one drawback to her wearing it. Yet he could deal with that fact for one evening.

He raised both his arms and waved at her, smiling when she waved back, cupped her hands around her mouth, and shouted, "We love you, Scottie!" He chuckled and snapped his chinstrap into place, but as he turned to watch the coach giving the team a final go-over of the play, his mind lingered on Jacey. Time was short. He felt it slipping away. He'd be leaving in less than a year. Had he waited long enough? Had he waited too long?

"Pendleton!" the coach shouted. "Get your head in the game!"

"Yes, Coach," Scott said. However, in that moment, in the moment before he put his mind on the game, Scott Pendleton made a decision. He'd waited long enough. He'd waited until sixteen. And sixteen had arrived. Yep. He'd waited long enough, and the waiting was over.

♥

"How was the game?" Mandy Whittaker asked as Jacey entered through the kitchen door.

"We won!" Jacey told her, forcing a smile.

"Good!" her mother said. "Did Scott do well?"

"Scott always does well, Mom. Three touchdowns tonight," Jacey said. "Everybody went to Drake's Drive-In after the game. The team was pretty pumped about the win."

"Didn't you want to go?" Mandy asked. "You could've called, and we would've let you stay out."

"I know," Jacey said. "But...but I'm just sort of tired. Just felt like coming home."

Mandy Whittaker's eyes narrowed as she looked at her daughter. It was heartbreaking having to watch Jacey go through the pain of unrequited love. The fact was, Mandy suspected the love Jacey felt for Scott wasn't as unrequited as Jacey thought. Mandy also suspected Scott was biding his time—waiting—waiting for Jacey to grow up a bit.

Still, Jacey's misery had become more and more apparent. Not to everyone perhaps, but to Mandy it was painfully obvious. First love was a mean dog. No one ever completely got over it. But Mandy knew it was part of life, a part of life everyone had to endure... even her precious daughter.

"Scott gave you his jersey?" Mandy asked, stating the obvious.

"Yeah," Jacey said, tugging at the hem. "He said I needed to show my school spirit."

"Looks to me like he wanted to show the school something," Mandy said, winking at her daughter. "Nothing shows ownership like a football jersey."

"Don't I only wish," Jacey said, giggling. Jacey's mom had always had a knack for giving Jacey hope. However false it may have been, hope was always preferable to no hope.

"It's only ten," Mandy said. "Are you going to bed already?"

"Naw," Jacey sighed, kicking off her shoes. "Just thought I'd hang out a while…maybe read."

"Okay, sweetie," Mandy said, kissing Jacey lovingly on the cheek. "Sleep tight."

"Thanks, Mom. Good night," Jacey said, returning her mother's kiss.

Once in her room, Jacey melted. Tears filled her eyes. She felt defeated, tired, and alone. She needed a good cry but felt too tired to deal with one. A shower, some peanut butter, and a chocolate bar would have to do the trick instead.

Jacey opened the top drawer of her vanity and took out the small jar of peanut butter hidden there, noting she was down to two chocolate bars. Enough to get her through the melancholy of one night perhaps, but she would have to remember to put chocolate bars on the grocery list under the fridge magnet next time she went downstairs.

Unwrapping one of the chocolate bars, she broke a corner from it and opened the peanut butter jar. Plunging in the bit of chocolate, she withdrew it heaping with the delicious, sticky mess, stuffing it in her mouth as she pushed play on her CD player and began to undress.

In the serene isolation of Jacey's bedroom, Donny Osmond was thirteen again and crooning "I'm Your Puppet." Jacey stepped into the shower, and after a warm, refreshing rinse, Jacey did feel much better. She put on her underwear monogrammed "Monday," even though it was Friday, and just to make herself more emotionally miserable, she pulled Scott's jersey on as a nightgown.

After another corner of chocolate blobbed in peanut butter, Jacey dried her hair. Humming softly to herself, she programmed the CD player to repeat Donny's version of "Too Young."

"That should do it," she said to herself as the music began.

Jacey smiled, grateful her mother had been a die-hard Donny Osmond fan as a teenager—for he indeed had a beautiful voice as a boy, not to mention as an adult. She was glad her mom had continued to listen to her old Donny Osmond music when Jacey was little—glad her mom listened to his newer material too and appreciated such a talented vocalist. Both Donny and Elvis gave Jacey the venues to either really wallow in melancholy or dream the happiest daydreams. She loved the smooth perfection of Donny's voice, the sultry southern warmth of Elvis's, and often wondered if she hadn't been born a couple of decades too late.

Another bite of chocolate and peanut butter, Donny singing "Puppy Love" repeated a few times, and Jacey found her spirits began to lift somewhat. She tried not to think of Scott, tried not to imagine him at Drake's, girls dripping from his elbows. It hurt to think of it, and Jacey was tired.

"Come in," she said as she heard a knock on her bedroom door. Expecting to see her mother enter, Jacey gasped as she turned to see Scott open the bedroom door and step into her private domain. Not that he hadn't been in her room before, but this night was different. This night it was her sanctuary, her hiding place. Not to mention she had no makeup on and still wore his football jersey.

"Hey, sugar britches," Scott said, smiling at her as he studied her from head to toe. "Whatcha doin'?"

"Getting read for bed," she told him, blushing crimson. "What are you doing here? Didn't you go to Drake's?"

Scott shrugged and picked up the peanut butter jar, dipping his index finger into it and popping his finger into his mouth next.

"I went for a while…but you never showed up," he said.

Jacey shook her head at him and handed him a piece of chocolate bar. "Oh, so you came home just because of me?" she teased, although her heart raced with the hope he might actually be serious.

He dipped the chocolate in the peanut butter and nodded as he ate it. "Yeah," he said.

"Oh, right!" Jacey exclaimed. Her heart was beating furiously, and she suddenly had the desire to drop to her knees before Scott and beg him to love her. "You're eating all my peanut butter," she teased, taking the jar away from him and setting it back on the vanity.

"I don't want you going out with Chris Santore, Jacey," he stated unexpectedly.

"What?" Jacey asked, rather astonished at the force of the statement. "Why not?" she said, picking up a bottle of fruit-scented lotion from the vanity and squeezing a dollop in one hand. "He's your friend. You told me yourself he's a nice guy." Jacey sat down at her dressing table as she smoothed the lotion over her arms, grimacing as she looked at her reflection. Inside her mind was going crazy with reasons why Scott would not want her going out with Chris. Was he jealous? She shook her head at the preposterous notion. Sure. Scott Pendleton jealous of another guy? And where Jacey was concerned? Right. Most likely Scott thought Chris was what was commonly known as a "man-hoochie," meaning he liked to make out with every girl he could get his hands on. Jacey smiled, touched Scott would take the time to look out for her…even if it weren't for his own reasons.

"Yeah…but…I just don't think you should," he told her. "Who's this?" he asked, momentarily distracted by the song playing on the CD player. "This isn't Donny Osmond, is it? Again?" He smiled and shook his head. "You know you're the only sixteen-year-old girl on the face of the earth who—"

"Do not dis Donny, Scott," Jacey scolded, shaking her hairbrush at him. "Do not dis one of the greatest voices on the face of the earth." Scott smiled, and Jacey knew he was trying not to laugh. He knew how seriously she took her favorite singer. "And yet…because I love you," she began, standing and going to the CD player, "but mostly because I love Donny and will not have him mocked…" She pressed stop on the CD player.

Opening it, she removed the CD, replacing it with another. "I'll change the CD for you." Jacey returned to her seat at the dressing table and began brushing her hair. Scott smiled, sighed, and rolled his eyes as Elvis singing "Love Me" wafted from the CD player.

"No eye-rolling, Scott," Jacey said, looking at him from the mirror and shaking her hairbrush in his direction. "Don't you mock my Elvis either."

"I suppose you set it on repeat too," he chuckled.

"Of course," she admitted. She was nervous, trembling. Something was different. Jacey had spent years in Scott's presence, yet with each passing day it seemed he unsettled her, delighted her, more and more. She was quickly reaching the point of losing control and melting into a mess, confessing her love for him— her heartache at not owning him.

She straightened in her chair and tried to appear unaffected as he continued, "Anyway, I don't think you should go out with Chris tomorrow night."

"Give me a good reason," Jacey told him. "I don't think you should go out with Liz Robertson tomorrow night either…but…but…"

Scott frowned and asked, "What do you mean? Why do you think I shouldn't go out with Liz?"

Jacey looked at him from the mirror reflection, and Scott saw something pass over her face—something that gave him hope. What he read in her expression… was it concern, jealousy, hurt? He couldn't quite make it out, but whatever it was, it gave him hope and the courage to continue on the path he'd decided to take.

"Because…because…she's not right for you," Jacey told him finally. It took every ounce of courage for her to say what she thought of Liz. Would he be angry with her?

"Not right for me? I'm eighteen years old, Jacey. What makes you think I'm looking for whoever's right for me? At…at this age…we're just having fun. Right?" he said.

"Well…well, I'm just having fun too, and you said Chris was a nice guy," she stammered. She wondered if she should turn and face him—tell him how she felt about him. Tell him she didn't want to go out with Chris, that she only wanted him—that she only wanted Scott Pendleton.

"He *is* a nice guy," Scott admitted. "It's just that… he's a guy."

"And what do you mean by that? Do you think I don't know about guys?" Jacey said, continuing to brush her hair. Her hands trembled, and she hoped he didn't notice.

"I…I…think you *think* you know about guys," Scott admitted. Jacey saw him glance over to her bed, piled high with nearly every stuffed animal Scott had ever given her over the years. Even, and she watched him grin when he saw it, the raggedy old rabbit he'd given her when she turned five. She'd dragged the rabbit everywhere and used to chew on one ear.

"I hope you've washed this thing a few times," he said, reaching out and picking up the well-worn bunny.

"Remember how you used to wipe your nose on it and—"

"Be quiet!" Jacey said, fairly leaping from her chair and snatching the bunny from his hands. "I can handle myself with Chris, Scott," she said as she lovingly placed the bunny back on her bed. "You don't need to worry about it." She paused, and her eyes widened. "Unless there's something you haven't told me about him."

Scott smiled. He loved when Jacey's imagination began to run away with her. Her eyes would always widen with the anticipation of what horrors she might learn. He loved the way her hair fell down around her shoulders, the radiance that shone in her face even at the end of the day. He loved the way she looked wearing his beat-up old football jersey. He wondered what it would feel like to hold her next to him when she was wearing it.

He swallowed hard and blinked away the dramatic emotions he was feeling toward Jacey. He'd always adored her—always loved her. Elvis crooning about sultry, pleading romance didn't help calm him either.

"There ain't nothing to tell," he managed finally. "He's a good guy…I guess."

Oh, how Jacey wished Scott's concern about her going out with Chris sprang from jealousy! Oh, how she wished he'd take her in his arms and say, *I want you for myself. That's why I don't want you going out with Chris Santore.* But she knew her dreams of Scott Pendleton were only that—dreams.

"Just don't let him kiss you," Scott added, reaching out and putting one hand at her waist. Jacey put her hand on his shoulder as he took her other hand in his free one. His feet moved slowly as he began to dance with her. Jacey smiled. She loved the feel of his hand at her waist, and she had always loved dancing with Scott. Ever since their mothers had signed them up for ballroom dance classes five summers before, Jacey had loved dancing with Scott. Of course, they were both teenagers now, and it wasn't long before he drew her hand to rest with his against his chest, pulling her against him and swaying slightly side-to-side. Scott winked at her, and she smiled when he said, "Just don't let him kiss you."

Jacey couldn't stifle a giggle, delighted he seemed to care whom she kissed. "Don't you kiss girls on the first date?" she asked, though the thought of Scott kissing another girl made her want to scream and burst into tears.

"That's not what I'm talking about," Scott said. He sang with Elvis as they danced.

Suddenly, Jacey felt as if she might pass out. Her heart was hammering far too hard in her chest, her skin felt hot, and her eyes threatened to fill with tears. Though he hid it, Scott had a fabulous singing voice. And his hand at her waist, his nearness, the low light of the room, his singing her favorite Elvis song—all of it was combining to perfectly break Jacey's heart.

He continued to sing with Elvis. Jacey tried not to stare at his mouth as he sang, tried not to wish he would be the first boy to kiss her…tried not to wish he would be the last.

"Come on," she breathed, desperate to distract herself. "You're putting up a double standard here. Are you going try and tell me that…that you're not going to try and kiss Liz tomorrow night?" She glanced down, not wanting him to see the excess moisture gathering in her eyes at the thought.

"That's my point, Jacey," Scott said. "Just because I'm going out with her doesn't mean…"

"Well, just because I'm going out with Chris… doesn't mean…" she stammered, but Scott had pulled her closer, flush with his body as they danced, until she was completely enfolded in his arms. He'd grown so much over the past two years. The top of Jacey's head barely reached his chin now, and suddenly she began to feel intimidated by his height, frightened somehow and very, very vulnerable.

"I'm just asking you not to let him kiss you," he said. She looked up to him, expecting to see his familiar teasing expression. The familiar expression of mischief was not on his face, however, and she was even more undone. His eyes had narrowed, his jaw was set firm, and his mouth was tight, his expression that of irritation.

"Okay," she sheepishly agreed. "But—but why not? If I like him and we have a good time…"

"Would it be your first kiss, Jacey?" he asked unexpectedly. Jacey was caught completely unprepared. She didn't want to appear foolish and naive in front of him, but she didn't see a good reason to lie to her best friend either.

"Um…um…yeah," she admitted.

Scott sighed and closed his eyes for a moment. He seemed simultaneously relieved and rattled. "Then don't let him kiss you," he rather ordered.

"But…why not?" she asked. Jacey had no intention of letting Chris Santore kiss her, yet Scott's interest in the matter had far more than merely piqued her interest. Her heart hammered, and her body tingled from his touch as she ventured, "Somebody's going to kiss me first someday. At least, I hope someone will."

"Yeah," he said. "Me." Jacey stopped breathing, her arms and legs bursting into goose bumps, the butterflies in her stomach suddenly multiplying a hundredfold.

"Scott…you're teasing me, and I don't think it's very funny," she said. Surely he was teasing her. Surely he did not mean it. Yet every fiber of her being hoped he did.

"I'm not teasing," he mumbled, taking her face in his hands. Jacey was surprised at the way her mouth suddenly grew hot and began to water. She couldn't tear her gaze from his perfect face, held her breath again when his thumbs traveled over her lips.

"Don't let him kiss you, Jacey," he whispered. "Don't ever let anybody kiss you…anybody but me."

Jacey's heart beat with such force in her chest it was nearly painful. She felt like crying, laughing, sobbing, all at the same time. Tears gathered in her eyes as she looked up at him. Could he really be serious? Was he telling her he cared for her? Cared for her as more than just a childhood friend?

"R-really?" Jacey stammered. It couldn't be! It was the fabric of every one of Jacey's dreams: Scott's adoration, his love.

"Really," Scott whispered as he gazed down at her, his thumb caressing her cheek.

"Nobody? Ever?" she asked, unable to believe what was happening. She smiled as a tear escaped her eyes and trickled over her cheek and teased, "Not even Donny?"

Scott chuckled and shook his head. "He's married," he said.

Jacey nodded and breathed a giggle, saying, "Not even Elvis?"

"The king is dead, sexy angel," he said, brushing her other cheek with the back of his hand.

"Just you then?" she asked in a disbelieving whisper.

"Just me," he told her.

Jacey couldn't stop more tears from escaping her eyes and traveling over her cheeks as she whispered, "Okay then."

"Okay then," Scott whispered. "And now that it's understood," he whispered as, for the very first time, Scott kissed her. A young lifetime of waiting ended; every "Kissing Scott Pendleton Dream" Jacey ever had was realized in that moment. The feel of his lips pressed to hers, the way his hands held her face, the scent of his cologne—faint at the end of the day—his soft whiskers on her cheek. All of it was magically dream-borne and perfect.

Carefully his arms wrapped around her body, pulling her tightly against him, and she let her hands be lost in the softness of his hair. It was plain he'd had more experience than she had, for he knew how to lead her into returning his kiss, and her shy, novitiate's manner soon gave way to a budding confidence. This was Scott, after all, her dream boy who owned her heart, as well as her best friend—starting running back on the varsity football team, voted best-looking by the senior class, perhaps—but her best friend all the same. She'd loved him for as long as she could remember, and now, somehow, she'd managed to capture his attention in the way she'd only dreamed of.

Scott sang in a whisper against her lips as Jacey's favorite Elvis song began anew. He kissed her again and then whispered, "Just love me, Jacey." Jacey felt another tear escape her eye, travel down her cheek, and mingle with their kiss.

They whispered in unison to the song—their lips still touching.

"I…I love you, Jace," Scott whispered, and Jacey gasped with emotion as his mouth took her own in a driven yet careful kiss. He kissed her over and over, each time the passion between them heightening. After several minutes, he broke the seal of their lips and said, "I've…I've been waiting a long, long time for this."

"*You've* been waiting a long time?" she exclaimed in a whisper. "I've been waiting my entire life!"

"Really?" he asked, taking her face between his hands and smiling at her.

Jacey felt ridiculous having melted into a mess of tears and emotion. She wiped at the tears on her cheeks, embarrassed at the outburst. "Yes, really," she told him, her breath catching in her throat.

He smiled, brushing more tears from her cheeks with his thumbs before pulling her tightly against him. He still swayed slightly in rhythm with the music, and her tears renewed as he whispered, "Just love me, Jacey."

"I do," Jacey whispered. "I've always loved you. I...I really can't remember a time when I didn't."

"I was afraid you'd...you'd tell me to take a hike," he mumbled.

"What?" Jacey exclaimed, looking up at him. "You've...you've got to be kidding me."

He smiled and shook his head as he moved a strand of hair from her face. "Nope. Been sweating it out since I was...about fourteen."

"What? You're still kidding me," Jacey told him.

"Nope," he told her. "My first day of high school football practice...four years ago. Coach asked me what jersey number I wanted...and I knew. I knew I'd wait until you were sixteen...let you grow up, maybe reach an age where your parents might approve of us, you know, dating. I decided that day four years ago, I'd wait 'til you were sixteen...then I'd take my shot." Jacey could only stare at him, stunned into blissful silence. He smiled and held her away from him a moment, studying the jersey she wore. "I started varsity my freshman year, you know."

"I...I know," Jacey managed.

"Well...this is the jersey Coach gave me that day. The day I decided you were gonna be mine," he said.

Jacey stood awestruck, gazing up into the deep blue of his eyes, the perfect pretty-boy masculinity of his face. Scott Pendleton was a dream, and in that moment, Jacey's dreams had all come true.

"Scott!" Jacey exclaimed, throwing her arms around his neck as he lifted her, spinning her around. "I love you so much! I thought you would only ever be a dream to me."

"So...so you're good with it then?" Scott asked, kissing the top of her head as he put her down. "You're good with me for...everything? Homecoming even?"

Jacey smiled. "Homecoming?" she giggled.

"Of course," he said, smiling at her. "Let's get those pumpkins sold so you can get that sexy angel dress at the mall you've been wanting."

Jacey smiled as she placed her palm against Scott's cheek. Many were the nights she'd lain in bed of late, dreaming of wearing the white sequin dress at the mall for Scott and only Scott.

Scott smiled and turned his face to kiss her palm. Putting her arms around his neck, she stood on the tips of her toes and kissed him softly on the lips. Instantly his arms were around her, his body leading hers to sway with his.

He again sang with Elvis a moment before he kissed

her again. Jacey knew there could never be anything in life that would ever match those moments, those wonderful moments when Scott had first kissed her, told her he loved her and why he'd chosen the number sixteen as his varsity football number.

"Your mom is gonna kill me…if I don't leave now," Scott sang, deviating from the original lyrics as he took her hands in his and kissed her once more. He smiled at her, took the woven leather bracelet off his wrist, the bracelet all the starting varsity football players wore, and slipped it onto hers. Another tear traveled down Jacey's face, for she knew the significance of the gift. Varsity players only gave their team bracelets to their steady girlfriends.

"You want it?" he asked, frowning.

Could he really think there would be any chance she would refuse it? "Of course," she told him. "I've always wanted it."

"Good. Then I'll explain to Liz why I won't be picking her up tomorrow night, and you explain to Chris why he won't be picking *you* up tomorrow night," he said.

"Okay," Jacey said, brushing a tear from her face and smiling at Scott. He leaned forward and kissed her quickly on the mouth.

"And there's more where *that* came from, sexy angel," he said with a wink before leaving, closing the door behind him as he left.

Jacey stood in her room, Elvis still singing "Love Me," unable to move for several moments. Could it have all really happened? Had she really won Scott? Would she wake up in the morning to find it had all been just a beautiful dream?

But when Scott kissed her as he held his pickup door open for her the next morning, Jacey smiled. It was real! Scott Pendleton was hers.

Scott took Jacey's hand and led her up the bleachers. As they sat together holding hands and watching the junior varsity football game, Scott would periodically draw Jacey's hand up to his mouth and kiss the back of it tenderly.

"So your good with me then?" he asked, smiling at her.

Jacey placed one hand on his cheek and said, "I've always been good with you, Scott Pendleton. Just… just love me."

Scott winked at her then, bent, kissed her tenderly on the lips, and whispered, "You bet, baby."

PART TWO

CHAPTER ONE

Sitting up in bed, Jacey Whittaker wiped the tears from her cheeks with the back of her hands. Wincing at the ache in her heart renewed by the painful, dreamed memory, she took a deep breath, tossed the covers aside, and got out of bed.

"What's up, Jacey?" Nora groggily asked, raising herself up on one elbow.

"Nothing, girl," Jacey lied. "Just a bad dream. Go back to sleep. It's only seven."

"You getting up for good?" Nora asked, lying back down and fluffing her pillow.

"I've got class at eight, and Professor Johnson will dock my grade if I'm late again," Jacey said.

"It's days like this when I wonder how anyone ever goes to college beyond a bachelor's," Nora grumbled.

"You said it," Jacey said as she shut the bathroom door.

Burying her face in her hands for a moment, Jacey tried to dispel the vision of Scott Pendleton dominating her thoughts. Brushing more tears from her cheeks, she frowned at her reflection in the mirror and whispered, "Jacey…get a grip."

It had been four years since she'd last seen Scott. Four years since he'd said good-bye and left. Four years since the worst day of Jacey's life. Four years and Jacey still marveled at how her heart ached whenever she thought of Scott. Marveled at how her mouth still watered for want of his kiss. Watered not for want of *a* kiss, for she'd been kissed since her relationship with Scott had ended, but watered for want of *Scott's* kiss.

Closing her eyes, she could almost feel his arms around her, almost sense the scent of his cologne, almost taste his mouth as her body, mind, and soul ached with residual heartbreak. Although her dreams of Scott were far less frequent than they'd once been, each one hurt as deeply as the last. Especially the ones that manifest perfectly vivid memories like the one she'd just had.

The night Scott had first kissed her, first confessed his love for her—that night had been one of the most defining moments of Jacey's young life. From that moment on, Jacey had changed. Oh, Scott had always been one of the most prominent people in her life up to that point, it was certain. Still, from that moment forward…well, Jacey had altered, grown up, learning of love and eventually of heartbreak at the hands of the handsome, wonderful Scott Pendleton.

Jacey sighed and glopped toothpaste on her toothbrush. She pushed her hair out of her face as she bent over the sink and began rather furiously brushing her teeth. Jacey hated the mornings she awoke thinking of Scott. It always seemed her mind could not leave his memory well enough alone for the rest of the day whenever they began with him. Invariably, on such days Jacey found herself trying not to think of him, which only caused her to think more of him. On days like these she spent a good amount of time trying to remember just how he had looked as a teenager, trying to imagine just how he might look at present, as a full-grown man. Memories always flooded back, washing over her like a bittersweet glass of raspberry lemonade and leaving an unhappy, burning ache in her bosom.

Furthermore, Jacey knew by the end of the day she'd wind up pulling out the "Scott Box." Jacey's Scott Box was an old Nike shoebox, which ironically had once belonged to Scott himself. Now it was filled with photos of Scott and other Scott Pendleton memorabilia. It was also a fact the Nike shoebox was just the miniature version of its cedar chest parent. Jacey's cedar chest at home in her parents' house was crammed full of Scott—photos of Scott, gifts he'd given her, clothing she'd once worn that had previously belonged to him, every little tangible memory imaginable. Jacey had kept so many bittersweetly cherished trinkets and treasures of Scott, they filled the entire chest. It remained at home, at the foot of her bed, her grandmother's handmade quilt folded lovingly and lying on top of it.

Yep. As she rinsed the toothpaste from her mouth, Jacey knew the end of the day would find her curled up on her bed sniffling as Elvis sang "Love Me" via the

CD player and weeping as she sorted through her Scott Box.

But why today? It was a question that frequented Jacey's mind whenever she awoke from dreams of Scott. What sparked the dreams? She wondered if perhaps days like these were anniversaries of a sort—dates on the calendar when significant things had happened in the past, dates her subconscious kept track of, rinsing her mind with melancholy when they came back around each year.

A vision of Scott in a black tux and Jacey in her white sequin-drenched homecoming formal began to appear in her mind. The piece of long-ago memory caused Jacey to wince, and she shook her head, determined to stay in the present. Yet as she lingered in the shower, the hot water washing over her, she could almost hear "Love Me," almost see Scott's face as he sang in unison with Elvis, almost feel his arms around her as they danced. Her senses could nearly experience the swish of her dress, could almost smell the scent of Scott's cologne.

Hurriedly Jacey finished showering, dried and styled her hair, threw on a pair of jeans and a shirt, and left the apartment. She smiled as she locked the apartment door behind her, amused by the sound of Nora's snoring. Nora only snored in the morning, and Jacey was glad, wondering how she would ever get any sleep otherwise. She adored Nora, adored her stringy blonde hair, her toothy grin, her fabulous sense of humor and love of life. Yet even Nora's snoring couldn't lift the melancholy clouds from the morning.

Jacey sighed and gazed up into the blue summer sky. She enjoyed taking courses in the summer. The enrollment in classes was smaller, the days cheerier. And besides, it kept her busy until autumn arrived and the world could really be enjoyed. Autumn would mean pumpkins and baking and colorful leaves, and at that moment Jacey looked forward to sneaking home for a weekend in October to sell pumpkins to the neighbor kids. She hoped her mom had been watering the patch regularly back home.

She thought back to that first October she'd officially been Scott's girlfriend—thought back to how much fun they'd had selling pumpkins from the pumpkin stand they'd built together. "Scott and Jacey's Pumpkin Stand" had been the talk of the neighborhood for nearly a week that year. They'd sold over fifty pumpkins and in only six days! Jacey had offered to split the profit with Scott, but he had insisted she use the money to buy the white formal she wanted for the homecoming dance.

Jacey sighed, marveling at the small things that had given her such great joy back then. How she wished young adult life held more of that—easy happiness. But college was tough, and so was the social life that went with it. Oh, Jacey had plenty of fun, and she'd dated a ton. She'd even endeavored to have a few steady relationships since breaking up with Scott, but they'd all ended for the same reason: Jacey couldn't quit comparing them to her first love.

"Hey, Jacey!"

Jacey's attention was drawn back to the moment at hand as Carla Woodman reached out and took hold of her arm.

"We doing pancakes at your place tonight?" Carla asked.

"Tonight?" Jacey asked. Carla was a peppy girl with a happy smile and the kindest manner. She had always reminded Jacey of Scott's mother, however, and it angered her for a moment to look at the girl who so closely resembled the woman who had broken Scott's father's heart.

"It's Friday," Carla reminded her. "It's your and Nora's turn to host the pancakes. Did you forget?"

Jacey smiled and said, "I didn't realize it was Friday already."

"Well, you guys better have at least two pounds of bacon at the ready! I'm already salivating at the thought of it. Mmm!" Carla said with a wink. "We'll all be over about six, okay?"

"Totally," Jacey said, the thought of bacon causing her mouth to water too.

"See ya," Carla said as she rather skipped away.

Jacey smiled and sighed. Pancake night was always fun. It would be a good thing to anticipate throughout the day. Jacey, Nora, Carla, and two other friends— Carla's roommates Megan and Steph—scheduled a pancake night every week. Once a week, the girls gathered at one apartment or the other to stuff themselves with homemade pancakes slathered in butter and maple syrup. A heaping helping of bacon made the meal even more decadent, and Jacey made a mental note to remind her to pick up an extra pound of bacon just in case the stocks were running low in the freezer.

As she turned and headed for class, she frowned, noting once again how much Carla looked like Scott's mother. The memory of the day Scott's mother left him and his father entered her mind then, and she felt the old heartache, the hurt and pain the woman's actions had caused her son and husband.

"Pull it up, Jacey!" Jacey scolded herself out loud. "It's in the past." Shaking her head and gritting her teeth with determination, Jacey made her way to class. Yet Scott lingered in her mind all day, seemed to hold her heart in his hand. After four years, Jacey Whittaker had still not gotten over her first love, and she truly feared she never would.

♥

"Uh-oh," Nora said as she entered the apartment to see Jacey folding laundry at the kitchen table. "You're having a Scott day, aren't you." It was a statement, not a question, and Jacey knew better than to entirely deny it.

"Maybe," Jacey said, haphazardly tossing socks into a smaller basket.

"Don't maybe me," Nora said. "Wearing that ratty old football jersey while you're doing laundry, red-eyed and weepy looking." Nora shook her head and added, "Not to mention falsetto Donny crooning in here from the CD player in the bedroom." Nora paused, and Jacey rolled her eyes as her friend nodded at her. "Yep. You're having a Scott day."

"This too will pass," Jacey sighed, picking up a sock that didn't make it into the basket when she'd tossed it.

"Let's get the Nike box out, a roll of toilet paper for our snot and tears, and get this over with, girlfriend," Nora said, a sympathetic grin softening her face.

"No time," Jacey said. "Carla and them will be here any minute."

Nora reached out and took Jacey's hand in her own. "You know it never passes until you've seen his picture and cried about it, Jacey."

Jacey smiled, as always astonished at her friend's understanding and patience.

"I've cried about it already," Jacey said. "But...the girls will be here soon, and there's no time for photos."

"There's always time for photos," Nora argued. She sighed and then said, "Let me go get just one. I know which one too."

"No, Nora," Jacey whined. "There isn't time, and anyway...I don't feel like—"

"Just one. There's time for one," Nora said, heading toward the bedroom. "I'll get the right one. Hold on a second."

Jacey shook her head and sighed. She felt tired—drained—as she put her folded clothes back into the laundry basket and set it aside. She went to the refrigerator and took out two pounds of bacon, the syrup, and the pancake batter she'd mixed earlier.

Plugging in the electric griddle, she sat down on the sofa in the front room and waited for Nora to return.

"I've got it!" Nora exclaimed as she returned. "This is one of my favorites! It'll do the trick."

Jacey smiled at her friend's beaming face, at the tears already apparent in Nora's eyes. Ever since Jacey had first told Nora of Scott, related the tale of first love found and then lost, Nora had been emotionally attached and wrapped up in the saga, as if she'd been there herself. Nora had shared many tears with Jacey over the past two years of being her roommate, and Jacey adored her all the more for it.

"This one," Nora said, plopping down beside Jacey on the sofa. "This one has always been one of my favorites." She handed the photograph to Jacey and asked, "Do you know why it's one of my favorites, Jacey?"

"Because Scott's so hot in it. Duh," Jacey said as she gazed down at the photograph. The photograph had been taken the first summer Jacey and Scott had been together. Scott's dad had taken them all to the lake, and it was nearly sunset.

Scott looked divine! He wore his orange board shorts and was looking at Jacey with a happy grin. His young body was bronzed from the summer sun, and his hair was mussed like a little boy's. Jacey loved the picture of Scott, but she'd never quite been able to reason why. He wasn't even looking directly at the camera, making it hard to fully appreciate his already rugged good looks.

Jacey shook her head and smiled. "I look like an idiot!" she told Nora. "No makeup, sunburned nose, and what was my mother thinking letting me buy that stupid purple bathing suit? And what a stupid expression! Plus…you can't even see Scott's face very well."

"That's why I like this photo," Nora said. "It's the fact he's looking at you…the way he's looking at you…the expression on his face. See? He loved you, Jacey. You can tell by the way he's looking at you in the photo. There you are, stupid purple bathing suit, red-faced idiot expression…looking the most part like a drowned rat. And yet…see the expression on his face? He loved you, Jacey." Nora said. "He really did love you." Jacey brushed a tear from her face and lovingly traced Scott's photographed face with her fingers. Nora took the photo from her and whispered, "I'm sure wherever he is…he still does."

Jacey wiped another tear from her face and stood up. "My mom said she heard he transferred from State."

"What?" Nora said. "When did you talk to your mom about Scott, and why didn't you tell me?"

"Yesterday," Jacey said, realizing then it must've been her mother's mentioning Scott on the phone the previous day that had sparked her dreams. "She said she saw his dad at the grocery store and that he told her Scott had decided to transfer to another college for his last year. I guess without the athletic scholarship… State was just too expensive."

Nora shook her head and said, "I can't believe you

didn't tell me. Is he fully recovered from his injury? Is he doing okay...I mean, without playing football and all?"

Jacey shrugged her shoulders, feeling sick as she thought of Scott's injury, his lost year of college, and his lost scholarship. She closed her eyes for a moment, the film footage of the injury during the previous football season replaying horrifically in her mind. She'd never forget watching the game on TV with her dad, watching Scott take the ball, dart in and out avoiding tackle after tackle, gain sixty yards, and then go down in the hard, brutal tackle that destroyed his college football career. With rumors of a Heisman Trophy, State's greatest running back, number twenty-one, Scott Pendleton had seen the end of his collegiate football career...of any football career.

Some correspondents had dubbed Pendleton a coward when the young hopeful had decided to quit the game as opposed to trying to come back. Others sang his praises, reporting he showed wisdom in choosing not to follow a career path that was often so shortlived and painful.

Regardless, Jacey had cried for weeks afterward, heartbroken for Scott and the loss of his dreams, frustrated she could not be with him during his recoveries from surgery, saddened as she thought of his college degree having to wait until he was healthier.

"I don't know," Jacey answered. "That's all his dad said. He was transferring credits."

"No wonder you're having a Scott day though,"

Nora said as she gazed at the photo. With a heavy sigh, Nora breathed, "Oh, how I love him."

Jacey smiled, amused at her friend's sentimentality. "Nora," Jacey said, "you've never even met him."

"I know," Nora said. "But he was a gorgeous boy! If he were around now and still just the age he was in this photo…I think I would definitely have been tempted to rob the cradle."

Jacey laughed and wiped the last Scott tear of the day from her cheek. "Put the photo back in the box, Nora," she said, "before you slobber all over it and ruin it forever."

"Okay," Nora said, heading toward the bedroom. "But I need to scan this into my computer so I can slobber on him whenever I want to."

"Nora!" Jacey exclaimed, feigning disapproval. "What would Harbine say?" Carl Harbine was Nora's boyfriend—a handsome fellow in his own right and the perfect match for Nora.

"He'd say I was silly and then kiss me," Nora laughed.

Jacey shook her head, smiling and knowing Harbine would do exactly that.

"Oh my heck!" Carla exclaimed as she entered the apartment by way of the front door. "I am a starving pig! Bring on the bacon!"

"Hey, Jacey!" Steph greeted as she and Megan stepped in behind Carla. "Nice outfit!"

Jacey looked down at the tattered football jersey

she still wore. "You guys know I do laundry on Friday!" Jacey said.

"I don't care what you wear," Megan said. "Let's just get things cooking. I'm starving too!"

"Nora signed you guys up for the Indentured Servant Sale, Jacey," Carla said.

"What?" Jacey exclaimed. "Oh, no! Carla...you know I hated that! Do we have to do it again this year?" Jacey hated the Indentured Servant Sale fundraiser the apartment complex had at the beginning of every fall semester. It was for a good cause, no doubt. Raising money for the local children's home Christmas party was indeed a worthy task. But Jacey hated the Indentured Servant Sale.

"Last year I ended up dressed up like a French maid and cleaning Harbine's disgusting apartment!" Jacey reminded her friends.

"Perhaps," Carla said. "But look at the wonderful fruits of your labor!"

"That's right!" Nora said, returning from replacing the photo of Scott and Jacey. "Harbine and I met and fell in love because he bought you last year, Jacey," Nora said. "And wasn't that all worth it?"

Jacey laughed and shook her head with delighted amusement. "Nora...he hadn't done dishes in a month when I went in there! And have you ever cleaned a bathroom in high heels?"

"But now he does his dishes every day because you brought Nora into his life," Steph said.

"That's because he doesn't want his apartment to

smell like a giant penicillin culture when he and Nora are making out over there," Jacey said, winking at her cherished roommate.

"Well, Harbine will be buying me this year," Nora giggled. "So you won't have to worry."

"Nope…not about Harbine, anyway," Jacey said.

"I saw Leonard Kendall licking his chops when you walked by this morning, however," Megan giggled.

"Sick, Megan!" Jacey exclaimed, her stomach churning with distaste at the very thought of Leonard Kendall.

Carla laughed and put a friendly arm around Jacey's shoulders. "Don't worry, Jacey," she said. "It'll be fun! And anyways, think of the kids."

"Blah, blah, blah," Jacey said, picking up a package of bacon and cutting it open with a knife.

"Yeah, Jacey," Nora said. "Think of the kids."

"Whatever, Nora," Jacey said, smiling. "You just better hope Harbine has enough cash to outbid Leonard for *you*!"

"I'll kill him if he doesn't," Nora said, slicing open the other package of bacon.

"Oh, he'll buy you, Nora," Jacey said, smiling at her friend. "He'll buy you. But if he had me dress up like a French maid…I don't think I want to know what you'll be dressing up like."

Nora dipped her fingers into the fishbowl on the counter and flicked water in Jacey's face. "You just fry the bacon, Jacey," Nora laughed. "It's what you're good at."

Jacey smiled, laughed, and shook her head, happy in the company of friends.

"Jacey! Donny is too retro for tonight," Carla called from the back room. She returned carrying the CD player. Plugging it into an outlet in the front area, she turned up the volume as a still retro but more current tune began to play.

All the girls began to sing along as the scent and sizzle of bacon filled the air of the apartment.

Jacey smiled, happy for the moment. Scott still lingered in her mind and heart, as always. But pancake night with her friends was a nice reprieve, and she was determined to enjoy it. Scott would come to her again in her dreams, but for now she would try to live in the moment and hope for a future void of so much regret and heartache.

♥

The pancakes and bacon were delicious, and each girl ate until she was too full and completely uncomfortable. After a few hands of cards, however, the young women were feeling refreshed and energetic once more.

"Oh, wait! I love this song!" Jacey squealed as one of her favorite dance tunes began playing on the radio.

"Jacey! At least close the kitchen curtains!" Nora laughed as Jacey hopped up onto the kitchen table and began to sway her hips in time with the music. "I'm the One You Want" was one of Jacey's favorite songs! Slow, sultry, and sung in a breathless voice, in Jacey's mind it demanded a similar style in dance.

"*I'm the one you want,*" Jacey began singing as the song played. "*And you know it...don't deny it!*"

"*I'm the one you want,*" Nora and Carla joined in, each grabbing a wooden spoon and singing into it as if it were a microphone. "*And you know it...you won't get by it!*"

"*Kiss me, I'm yours. Don't miss me,*" Steph and Megan joined in as the song continued. Jacey stayed where she was, dancing on the table, slowly swaying and giggling along with the others.

"*I'm the one you want,*" all the girls sang as Jacey continued to dance. "*And you know it...don't deny it!*"

When the apartment door opened and Harbine walked in, not one girl seemed to be fazed by his presence.

"*I'm the one you want,*" the girls sang as a smile spread across Harbine's face. "*So kiss me. You don't wanna miss me!*"

Jacey couldn't help but smile at the sight of Harbine. His sloppy clothes and rather rotund physique gave him the look of a cuddly teddy bear. He ran his fingers through his already tousled blond hair and chuckled, "Looks like I'm in the right place at the right time!" He leaned forward and kissed Nora, and for some reason the sweet, natural act caused a sharp pain to prick at Jacey's heart. She turned away, continuing to dance but unable somehow to comfortably watch Harbine and Nora's affectionate exchanges.

"Hey, baby," Nora said. "I thought you had a late class tonight."

"I did," Harbine said. "But the prof let us out early. Good thing too," he continued, "'cause this guy wasn't sure which apartment was yours. You table-dancing hoochies really should put that number back on the door."

"What guy wasn't sure which apartment was ours?" Jacey heard Nora ask, still unwilling to turn around and watch two people in love interact with each other.

"This guy," Harbine said. Jacey instantly stopped dancing as she felt the hair on the back of her neck prickle. "He's looking for Jacey."

"Oh my hell!" Nora's astonished whisper caused Jacey's nerves to tighten.

"I bet you never expected to find her table dancing in her pajamas, did you, dude?" Harbine said.

"Nope," Jacey heard a low, masculine voice respond.

Swallowing hard and trying to still her trembling knees, Jacey turned around to see whom Harbine had brought with him, though something deep in her soul already knew.

CHAPTER TWO

"Hi, Jace," Scott said as Jacey stood staring down at him in disbelief. He was no less than entirely, completely, astonishingly magnificent! He wore an amused grin as he looked up at her, and she figured he'd grown at least three inches since she'd last seen him. The expanse of his shoulders was much broader than what it had been four years previously, and his perfect musculature was apparent even for his jeans and somewhat tight T-shirt. His jaw was squared, his face wider, his eyebrows thicker, and his hands larger, rougher—the hands of a man instead of a teenage boy. For all the ruggedness of his maturity, for all the awesome attractiveness of his face and form, his eyes, however, were the same—dark blue mirrors, accentuated by thick, dark lashes—and they melted Jacey's heart.

"H-hello," she managed to respond. Carefully, for her legs, her arms, and her entire body were trembling, Jacey stepped from the table onto a chair and then down to the floor.

"Still dancing on tables, I see," Scott said. His voice

was deeper but still held the same sultry intonation it always had.

"I...I guess," Jacey managed. She was uncomfortable, mortified with embarrassment as he studied her from head to toe, an amused grin spreading across his gorgeous face. It was then she remembered what she was wearing, and she wanted to shrink away and disappear into the floor. She could only imagine what he was thinking, finding her still wearing his old jersey after four years.

"Oh my hell," Nora whispered again.

"Quit swearing, Nora! Potty mouth," Carla scolded quietly, for everyone seemed to suddenly sense the discomfort Jacey was embroiled in.

"So," Harbine began, turning to face Scott. Silence never tarried long when Harbine was about. "I'm Harbine. Carl Harbine," he said, extending a hand to Scott.

"What's up?" Scott asked, shaking Harbine's hand firmly. "I'm Scott—"

"Dude!" Harbine exclaimed, his eyes lighting up like a Christmas tree. "Dude! You're Scott Pendleton! State's Scott Pendleton! I didn't recognize you. It's so dark outside. Dude! I love you!" Even Jacey couldn't stop from smiling at Harbine's excitement. "Jacey told me she grew up near you...but I—dude, Jacey!" Harbine laughed. "You're awesome, Jacey!" Harbine turned back to Scott. "Dude, I was, like, devastated when you got hurt, man. You're my hero."

"Not anymore, I guess, huh?" Scott chuckled. He

glanced at Jacey for a moment, winking at her as if to say, *Just a moment. Let me cool this guy down first.*

"Are you kidding, dude?" Harbine exclaimed. "More than ever! I mean—that tackle you took! Man, your leg was, like—crack! Crack, crack, cccccrrrrraaaaccckkkk! Dude...*I* limped for a week after seeing that! You're incredible, man. Incredible." Harbine stood, shaking his head in amazed awe.

"I...I...uh," Jacey mumbled, making to move past Scott and Harbine. "I'll be right back."

But when Scott reached out and took hold of her arm, she stopped as every inch of her flesh bubbled with delighted goose bumps.

She looked up to him as dropped his voice and said, "You're not even gonna talk to me?"

Jacey felt like screaming, sobbing, fainting as she looked up to him. "I...I'm just...just not dressed for company."

Scott's brow wrinkled as he looked at the group of people, including another man.

"Dude, Jacey," Harbine said to her. "You're hardly ever dressed when I'm over. What are you talking about?" Turning his attention back to Scott, he added, "Dude, Friday is Jacey's laundry day...and that old rag she's wearing is her laundry dress, I guess...'cause she wears it every time."

"Harbine!" Nora scolded in a whisper. "Will you shut up?"

"Dude, Nora!" Harbine exclaimed, however. "Scott Pendleton is in the house! How can I shut up?"

Nora put a hand to her forehead and shook her head. Jacey only silently begged for Scott to release his grip on her arm. His touch was undoing every sensible, rational instinct about her.

"Dude," Harbine said to Scott then, "you gonna be here for a few minutes?"

Scott's eyes narrowed as he looked at Jacey. "I hope," he said.

"Cool!" Harbine exclaimed. "If I go to my apartment—it's not far—and get my camera—dude, I have to have a picture of us together! And will you sign something for me?" Harbine rattled on. "It's an old State football I caught at one of your games once."

Scott smiled at the exuberant fan. "Sure," he agreed. "But…but it won't be worth much…anymore."

Harbine shook his head, put his hands on Scott's shoulders, and stared at him with the most serious of expressions. "Priceless to me, dude. Priceless."

"Go get your ball, man," Scott said, chuckling.

"Awesome!" Harbine exclaimed as he bolted out the door.

"Well, I guess we'll be on our way, Nora," Carla said, taking Steph's and Megan's hands in her own and leading them toward the door.

"Oh, no, no. Don't go on account of my intrusion, ladies," Scott said, still gripping Jacey's arm firmly in one hand.

"We were just leaving when you arrived anyway," Steph lied. "It was nice to meet you."

"You too," Scott said as the girls left. "You ladies have a nice evening."

"I really should walk with Harbine," Nora said as she too headed for the door.

"Nora?" Jacey breathed, afraid to be left alone with Scott, afraid she would melt at his feet in a puddle of confused, astonished, heartbroken tears.

"We'll be right back," Nora said, closing the door behind her.

"Wow," Scott said, finally releasing Jacey's arm. "I guess I can really clear a room."

"Oh, it's not you," Jacey stammered. "It's…it's Harbine. He's just so…enthusiastic about stuff. People get a little worn out around him sometimes."

"I'll pretend I'm buying that," Scott said, smiling at Jacey as she stood utterly undone before him.

He smiled as he looked her up and down again. Taking hold of the shoulders of the old jersey, he tugged at it and said, "In the end…reduced to the laundry day togs, huh?" His touch, no matter how casual, how light, was nearly unbearable! In those moments, Jacey wondered if she would ever recover from seeing him again, for her heart, her mind, her body…her very being was in turmoil! A sort of pleasurable turmoil borne of misery.

"Gotta wear something while I'm doing my laundry," was all she could manage.

He shrugged his shoulders and said, "I guess…if you're a girl anyway." Jacey was instantly melancholy, all too familiar with his baiting, teasing ways. Still, for old time's sake, she decided to fall for it.

"Well…what do you wear when you're doing laundry, Scott?" she asked. The feel of his name in her mouth made it start to water.

"Not much," he said, smiling and winking at her. She couldn't help but smile, delighted by his teasing manner.

"You're still funny, I see," she told him.

He chuckled and said, "And I still do my laundry in my underpants."

The ice had been broken, and although Jacey was still uncomfortable, still fighting the feeling her heart may dissolve and bleed out of her body somehow, she smiled at him—smiled at the boy, the man, who would always be her first love.

"How are you?" she asked.

Scott exhaled heavily, shrugged his shoulders, and sighed, "Okay."

"Really?" Jacey asked. "I…I was worried for you after your injury…your choice not to play anymore. I know it must've been hard on you. I know how much you wanted it."

Shrugging his shoulders again, he said, "It's not the only thing I ever wanted. It's not even the thing I wanted the most. So…it's okay. I'm good with it."

"I'm glad to hear that," Jacey said, even though she suspected he was covering up his true feelings. "And your injury? Is it all better?"

Scott nodded and squeezed his thigh. "Broke the leg

in three places and tore the ACL. But it's all good now."
He looked at her and grinned, and Jacey thought she
might pass out cold from the thrill traveling through
her body. He was fabulous! Not simply physically
gorgeous but wonderful in every meaning of the word.
Jacey hated herself for not being able to hold onto him.

"How…how are you doing?" he asked her then.

Jacey smiled and said, "Well, I certainly don't have
the adventures to tell that you do!"

"Well, that's a good thing," he said, smiling.

Jacey shook her head, suddenly realizing how rude
she must seem by not having offered him a seat. "Come
on over and sit down," she said, motioning to the sofa
as he followed her. Once he'd settled on the sofa, Jacey
sat in the chair across from him. She tucked the hem of
the jersey tightly around her thighs, ensuring modesty.

"No adventures?" he asked. His eyes seemed to
smolder with mischief and daring—and an emotion
Jacey couldn't quite identify.

"Not really," Jacey said, shrugging her shoulders.

"Well, after meeting your friend Harbine…I have a
hard time believing that," he said.

Jacey giggled at the thought of Harbine. "He is
hilarious, isn't he?" she asked.

"Yep," Scott said. "He's your roommate's boyfriend?"

"Yeah. He bought me at the servant sale last
autumn, and they hooked up pretty soon after," Jacey
explained.

"He…he bought you at a servant sale?" Scott asked,
smiling, obviously amused.

"Yeah, he did," Jacey answered, smiling at the memory. "It's a fundraiser the apartment complex has—an indentured servant thing. The guys pay for half a week of a girl's servitude, the girls pay for half a week of a guy's. All on the up and up...no hanky-panky, of course."

"Oh, of course," Scott chuckled.

"Harbine bid on me and won. He made me wear a little French maid uniform—completely modest, naturally."

"Naturally," Scott said, still smiling.

"And he had me spend three days cleaning his apartment...in high heels. But I guess it was all worth it 'cause by the end of the week, he and Nora were... you know..."

"A couple," he finished for her.

"Yeah," Jacey said. "Our friend Carla—she was here when you first got here—she signed me and Nora up for sale again this year. But...at least I know I won't be working for Harbine this time."

Jacey blushed as Scott smiled and looked her up and down again.

"Blah, blah, blah," she said. "I'm sure you wanted to know all that."

"I did," he said.

"So...what brings you here?" she asked him then. *Please, please, please say it was me!* she thought.

"I lost my scholarship at State when I decided not to play anymore," he began, "and after losing out on two semesters because of the injury, I decided to transfer. So I—"

"Dude! Check it out!" Harbine exclaimed, bursting through the door, Nora on one arm, a football on the other, and wearing a number twenty-one State football jersey. "I'm wearing the red and black, man! Your number!" Scott winked at Jacey as he began to chuckle. "Dude, Nora," Harbine said, handing her the football and pulling his camera out of his back pocket. "Hold this while I get some pictures." Harbine awkwardly pointed his camera in Scott and Jacey's direction. "Dude, Jacey," he said, "stand up with Scott. Let me take a practice shot. Then you can take one of me and him together."

Uncertain as to what else to do, Jacey stood up as Scott rose from the sofa.

"He's a scream," Scott whispered, smiling.

"He makes me scream sometimes," Jacey whispered in a giggle.

"Right there, man, right there," Harbine said as Scott moved to stand right next to Jacey. She stiffened when he put his arm around her shoulders. His touch, the warmth of him next to her, and the scent of his all-too-familiar cologne were overwhelming.

"Say, 'Sneeze,' kids," Harbine said. Jacey smiled, and Scott dropped his arm from around her after the camera flash dissipated.

"Unbelievable!" Harbine exclaimed. "I love you, Jacey! I love you for knowing this guy!"

Jacey glanced at Scott, shaking her head and smiling

with delight at the antics of her friend. He smiled at her, and her heart skipped several beats.

Looking back to Harbine, Jacey held out her hand and said, "Okay, Harbine…your turn." Harbine snapped one more quick photo before handing her the camera.

"Awesome!" Harbine exclaimed, clapping his hands together hard once to display his exuberance.

Jacey and Nora both giggled as Harbine stepped up next to Scott, straightened his shoulders, and puffed out his chest.

"Dude, Jacey," he said, "try to make me look hot."

Jacey giggled, and Nora said, "Honey, you couldn't be any hotter if you tried."

Looking through the camera view window, Jacey felt her smile fade and felt tears begin to well in her eyes. Scott was incredible! As incredible as he'd always been. More so, and it hurt to see him, to have him so near and not be able to…to have him.

Once Jacey had taken no less than twenty photos of Harbine and Scott together, Harbine trotted over to her and said, "Let me see. Did they all come out?" He reviewed the digital photos stored on his camera before laughing and announcing, "Awesome!" Retrieving the football from Nora, he took it to Scott, withdrawing a pen from his pocket and asked, "Do you mind?"

Scott chuckled, "Not at all, dude. It makes me feel like I'm somebody."

Jacey frowned. His lip service of how he'd given up football and didn't really care was just that—lip service.

Still, football hadn't made him somebody. God had made him somebody, and he still was.

"You know," Scott began as Harbine looked at his autographed football and mouthed, *Awesome!* several times in succession. "I've got something for you, man."

"For me?" Harbine asked. "What's that?"

"I mean…if you want it," Scott said.

"Dude! I'm sure I want it! What is it?" Harbine asked, his eyes twinkling like an excited child's.

"I mean…you seem like you…I don't know. It's probably stupid," Scott said, seeming to change his mind.

"No, dude. Serious," Harbine prodded. "What is it? I'm sure I want it."

"It's dumb…but…I know some people collect them," Scott stammered.

Harbine took Scott by the shoulders. "Dude, we're buddies now, man. You can give me anything."

Jacey smiled as Scott shook his head and laughed. "Do you…do you…do you want one of my football jerseys? I mean, I don't know what you wear to do your laundry in, but a jersey seems to suit Jacey…and since you seem to like football and all…I just thought you might—"

"Dude!" Harbine said, slapping Scott's shoulders hard. "Are you serious? I mean…seriously? Would you give me a jersey? Like…an official collegiate football jersey? I mean, do you have one you wore in a game? Dude! I would die a happy man if I could snarf one of them off you!"

"Man…you're too cool!" Scott chuckled. "I've got one at my apartment. It's still packed, but I can get to it pretty easy. If you want it. Then maybe you and Jacey can both have a laundry jersey."

"Dude, Jacey!" Harbine said, looking at Jacey like he'd never seen her before. "Jacey! Is that old rag a Scott Pendleton jersey? Like…high school?"

"Yes," Jacey said, frowning.

"Girl! You wear that for doing laundry? It should be framed or something!" Harbine exclaimed, obviously mortified Jacey should defile the garment.

"Dude, I'll get you a jersey," Scott said, smiling at Harbine. "Just drop by my apartment tomorrow sometime…and we'll dig it out."

Jacey felt a wave of heat wash over her as Harbine said, "Dude…are you saying you live here?"

"Yeah," Scott said. "I transferred from State. Starting September, I'll finish my degree here. I'm up at Tannajuan right now, for two weeks before fall semester starts. I gotta find another place before then."

"Dude!" Harbine breathed. "Look no further, man! Your new roommate and best buddy is standing before you now."

"What?" Jacey said.

"Simon is moving at semester, Jacey," Nora said, finally able to get a word in. "Harbine is looking for a new roommate."

"Cool," Scott said, nodding at Harbine. "You sure?" he asked.

"Oh, yeah!" Harbine said, nodding. Then with

a sigh, he turned to Jacey, took her face between his hands, and kissed her hard on the mouth. "You, my dear...are an angel! Stinkin' Scott Pendleton is going to room with me, man!"

Jacey smiled as Harbine turned to Nora and said, "What a night, huh, baby?" He picked Nora up and spun her around a moment before kissing her several times in succession. "I'll tell you...that Jacey Whittaker of yours brings blessings into my life."

"You're a child, Carl Harbine!" Nora giggled.

"That's why you love me!" he said, kissing her again. He turned and nodded at Jacey and said, "Well, I'm off, dudes. I'll drop by Tannajuan tomorrow for that jersey, man."

"Okay," Scott said. "I...uh...I better be going too," he added, following Harbine to the door. "I've been driving all day, and you girls probably need your rest." He smiled at Nora, nodded, and said, "Thanks for letting me interrupt your evening."

"Any time," Nora said, placing a friendly hand on his forearm.

He looked up at Jacey and smiled. "It was good to see you, Jace," he said. "I'm glad things are going well for you."

"You too," Jacey managed. She wanted to cry, to shout, *Don't leave!* But she didn't. He had revealed nothing to her. Did he intend to ever see her again, or would she simply have to hope for chance meetings on campus? Was he in love with anyone? If she did chance to meet him on campus, would she have to endure watching him with another woman? As she watched him close the door behind him, she did know one thing. One thing she knew for certain, and so did Nora.

"If he wanted you, you'd go back to him in a moment...under any terms, wouldn't you, Jacey?" Nora asked.

As tears began to stream over Jacey's cheeks, she whispered, "I would." She knew it as strongly as she ever had. If Scott ever decided he'd made a mistake, if there was ever a chance of having him for her own again...but she knew there never would be a chance. He'd explained it to her long ago, and she was certain he'd mean it now as much as he had then. Jacey was a part of his past; he'd moved on with his life. She would have to learn to live with it all over again. Jacey knew her broken heart—the heart she struggled so hard to salvage. Jacey knew the salvaging would have to begin again.

CHAPTER THREE

Three days passed. Three long days since Scott Pendleton had walked into Jacey's apartment and back into her life. Three days since she'd been able to really eat anything of consequence. Three nights since she'd been able to sleep.

Everywhere she went, Jacey found her eyes searching for Scott, praying for a chance encounter, hoping to catch a glimpse of him, be the beneficiary of one of his dazzling smiles. But she did not see him. And even if she had, she knew it would've done no good; it would just be the constant reminder of what was no longer hers.

However, Harbine's roommate, Simon, had finished up finals early and left, leaving room for Scott to move in early. Jacey knew she would see him, knew there would be no way of avoiding him—at least in going and coming from the complex at times. Her heart began to beat more rapidly whenever she thought of seeing him again, both with delight and trepidation.

He'd acted so...so casual when he'd come into the apartment that night. It almost seemed as if he were unaffected by what had happened between them so long ago. All of it, good or bad. Jacey was angry about his relaxed manner sometimes, his appearing so unaffected. Secretly she'd always hoped he'd been as miserable for as long as she had.

Nora was no help. She, being the perpetual optimist, had decided Scott had shown up in Jacey's life not by chance but for a reason. This only drove Jacey's thoughts in more irrational directions—down venues that were pointless.

Through it all, the three long days since she'd seen him, Jacey struggled to despise him somehow—to find fault with his character and appearance even though there was none. She tried not to see his gorgeous smile and beautiful eyes in her dreams, tried to remember how thoroughly he'd broken her heart. Yet in the end, she knew—she could never hate him. She'd tried for years to no avail. His return—strong, virile, mature, more handsome than ever before—only cemented her heart to being forever hardened and tarnished.

♥

"Scott's all moved in, Jacey," Nora said as she entered the apartment after her Tuesday classes. "Let's take cookies up to the guys."

"You take cookies up to Harbine if you want to, Nora," Jacey said, her heart racing at the knowledge Scott was only across the complex courtyard. "I...I don't have a good reason to go with you."

"What?" Nora exclaimed. "Jacey...you're the dumbest thing I know."

"Thanks," Jacey said, smiling at her friend.

"Scott is our newest neighbor," Nora said. "Haven't we always taken cookies to every new neighbor?"

"Yes, nag queen," Jacey said. "But this is different."

"No, it's not," Nora insisted. "And besides, he's your friend. You guys were completely amicable over here the other night."

"He was amicable. I was faking it," Jacey reminded her.

"But he doesn't know that," Nora said.

"You forget, Nora…he knows me. Therefore, I'm sure he knows that," Jacey said.

"Wake up, Jacey!" Nora exclaimed suddenly. "Heaven has given you guys a second chance! It's meant to be! Don't throw it away."

Jacey angrily wiped at a tear unexpectedly escaping her eye. "If heaven is giving me a chance at anything… it's a chance to face him again so that I can finally move on."

"Well, then, if that's what you think…then do it," Nora stated. "There are still cookies left from the batch we made yesterday. Let's take some over. I'll give you a minute to get all spiffed up. Unless you want to just throw on that old jersey again and really let him know how much you still pine for him."

Nora was right. At least partially. If heaven or fate had brought Scott close at hand so Jacey could find some closure of some sort…then so be it.

"Okay," Jacey said, though she truly wondered if

she had the strength to face him again. "Give me a second to...to..."

"To buck up?" Nora offered.

"Yes, twerp!" Jacey said, unable to keep from smiling at her caring, concerned friend. Nora was a jewel. Jacey laughed as Nora's toothy smile triumphantly spread across her face.

"I'll get the cookies ready. You put on some lip gloss," Nora said, clapping her hands together with delight.

Ten minutes later, Jacey's body began to quiver as she and Nora stepped into Harbine and Scott's apartment.

"We brought cookies," Nora began, handing a plate of cookies to Scott. Harbine came bounding out of the back room like a puppy anticipating a doggie treat.

"Mmmm! Cookies!" Harbine said as he looked at the plate in Scott's hands.

"Your sugar is over this way, baby," Nora said, winking at Harbine and taking hold of his hand.

"Mmmm! Cake!" Harbine said as he drew Nora into his arms, kissing her ravenously.

Harbine and Nora's affectionate exchange left Jacey to explain the cookies to Scott.

"We...we always bring cookies to our new neighbors," she stammered. She found it difficult to look at him, for fear she would never be able to stop once she started.

"Cool," Scott said. "Thanks. Peanut butter?" he asked.

Jacey smiled, remembering peanut butter cookies were Scott's favorite. "Yes. Actually, they are."

"Awesome!" Scott said, smiling at her. Jacey smiled, amused at how Scott had begun to sound like Harbine after only a few days of being in his company. She stood awkward and uncomfortable as Harbine and Nora continued to kiss and whisper insinuative endearments to one another.

"Why don't you take a seat?" Scott said, pointing to the incredibly worn sofa in the front room of the apartment. "It…it looks like you might be here awhile."

Jacey's first inclination was to turn and run, to escape before too much time in Scott's company began to cause her heart to ache too brutally. However, she smiled and went to the sofa. She sat down and watched as Scott, still standing, peeled back the foil covering the cookies and began to eat one. As her heart did indeed begin to ache from simply being in his presence, Jacey looked about the apartment to try to distract herself. She smiled as she saw one of Scott's State football jerseys hanging sloppily on the wall.

Jacey smiled and glanced up at the large poster of Scott on the wall. She had one too, although hers remained safely rolled up in her closet at home. Jacey had given the Scott Pendleton poster to Harbine the previous summer for his birthday. She loved the poster of Scott in motion, breaking a tackle. She smiled as she saw the autographed football, carefully placed on a stand atop a nearby, and very ratty-looking, bookshelf.

Harbine's framed football game ticket stubs cluttered the wall nicely, as did several State pendants.

"Harbine's crazy," Scott said, following Jacey's gaze. "Look at all this stuff he hung up before I got here."

"It's always been here," Jacey said, "ever since Harbine moved in. Except the jersey you gave him. That's new."

"Really?" Scott said, his smile fading. "But I was just a…a football player."

"You were his favorite football player," Jacey reminded him. "I know Harbine…and you've made his dreams come true by moving in here." She smiled at him, touched at the way the man seemed to be able to fulfill people's dreams…or shatter them.

"He's a scream," Scott said, popping another cookie into his mouth.

"Do you think you can live with him though?" Jacey asked in a whisper, glancing over to make certain Harbine was still too involved with Nora to hear her.

Scott looked over his shoulder at his roommate too before hunkering down in front of Jacey and whispering, "He's a character, that's for sure." He smiled, however, ate another cookie, and added, "But he's got a good soul. And I like that." He chuckled, and the breeze from the open door blew his hair. "Still, I think I'll be having perpetual dish duty. I don't think he does them much." Jacey smiled, barely controlling the urge to reach out and run her fingers through his hair the way the breeze had.

"Believe me…if you don't want lab cultures

growing in your sink...*you* will have to do the dishes," she told him.

"Yeah," Scott said, still hunkering before her, still eating cookies. "He showed me the 'before' and 'after' pictures of his apartment before you cleaned it last fall."

"Unbelievable, wasn't it?" Jacey giggled.

"Unbelievable," Scott agreed. "I saw the ones of you too...in that nice little maid outfit. Nice!" he said with a wink. "The French maid thing works for you... and here I always thought you were just a sexy angel."

"You're going to get a stomachache," Jacey said, desperate to change the subject. He hadn't forgotten! He hadn't forgotten the "sexy angel" endearment, and his speaking it caused her heart to flutter. His eyes twinkled with mischief as he smiled at her.

"You're wiggin' out about Harbine showing me those pictures, aren't you?" he chuckled.

"Wouldn't...wouldn't you be?" she mumbled, feeling the crimson rising to her cheeks.

"Are you kidding?" he whispered. "How do you think I felt...walking in to find a lifesize poster of myself on the wall?"

"It's better than knowing Harbine is showing the entire world those pictures of me dressed up like an idiot," Jacey said, shaking her head as she watched Nora and Harbine still kissing at the front door.

"Oh, believe me," Scott chuckled, shaking his head. "You looked like anything but an idiot."

Jacey felt herself blushing again. Why couldn't she control herself in front of Scott? It had been four years, for Pete's sake! How could he possibly still have such an effect on her?

"You guys okay there?" Scott called, smiling as he looked at Nora and Harbine. "You…uh…need us to leave or anything?"

Jacey smiled as she looked at her roommate. Nora's eyes fairly sparkled with delight in Harbine's affection. It was amazing, Harbine's effect on Nora. Jacey saw Harbine as a good friend—a funny, eccentric, sloppy boy who made life a little brighter. But Nora was in love with him, and it was perfect.

"Oh, that's all right, dude," Harbine said, breaking from Nora for a moment. "We're headed out to the hill, anyway." The hill was the popular make-out spot for romantically involved students. Isolated and easily accessible by foot or any other means of transportation, it was the perfect place to sit and talk and for any other romantic dalliances.

"You're leaving?" Jacey asked, suddenly disturbed by the fact Nora and Harbine were planning to leave, planning to leave Jacey in the lone company of Scott.

"Yep," Nora said. "See you later." Before Jacey could even open her mouth to protest, Harbine and Nora had exited the apartment, closing the door behind them.

"Well," Scott said, raising his eyebrows, and Jacey nervously looked to him. "I guess that's that."

"Yeah," Jacey managed. "I should probably go too. I have some things—"

"Afraid I'm going to bring up the past, Jace?" Scott asked.

Of course she was afraid he was going to bring up the past! However, she was more afraid she might blurt out a shocking confession of still being in love with him should she linger.

"No. Of course not," she lied.

"Well, you should be," he said, his smile fading, a frown puckering his brow. "Because...actually...I did want to talk to you about that."

Jacey was furious! Furious at Nora for leaving her alone with her heart's greatest and perfectly unobtainable desire—furious at Harbine for using his fluffy teddy bear ways and big brown puppy-dog eyes to lure Nora away—furious at herself for even agreeing to bring the cookies over! She couldn't handle talking about the past. She couldn't! She would cry and lay too many of her secreted cards on the table. But in the end, she was trapped. If she stood up and fled, he'd know she still held feelings for him. If she stayed, could she endure his fabulous presence without melting into a puddle at his feet? Without pledging her eternal servitude to him if only he would try to love her?

"I...I know you'd probably rather not talk about it," Scott began. Jacey's eyes widened, and she drew in a deep breath to try and calm her rattled emotions and nerves. "But...but there's something...something I've always wanted you to understand."

"Scott," Jacey said, holding up her hand to try and stop him, "it...it was a long time ago. I understand that you needed to—"

"You don't understand," he interrupted. "There's

no way you could possibly have ever understood. Because…because you don't know…you don't know why I—"

"You were nineteen, Scott. You were in college," she interrupted. "I…I was just in high school and—"

"That had nothing to do with it." It was his turn to interrupt. "There were reasons, Jacey. Not age or college verses high school…or…or a lack of…of…of feeling."

Jacey was quiet. He had something to tell her, and she was certain she didn't want to hear it. Still, she knew he would have his say. She had the overwhelming feeling if she stood and tried to leave, he would detain her…physically if needs be. And so she nodded, and he continued.

He drew a deep breath and began, "My…my mom…you remember when she left my dad?"

Jacey nodded. How could she ever forget it? She vividly remembered the day Mrs. Pendleton left Mr. Pendleton. She remembered how devastated Scott was even though his parents had been struggling for over a year. It was miserable, deeply sad, and Jacey had cried with her beloved Scott, tried to console him as best she could. Still, it had hurt and damaged him, and she had always wondered if his mother's leaving him and his dad had something to do with Scott breaking up with her. After all, he'd broken up with her only a week later. Still, she didn't want to relive any of it. Not Scott's pain at his mother's abandonment nor her own pain at his. She didn't want to hear his reasons. Already her heart was aching, had been aching since the night he'd stepped into her life again, and she did not want to relive the pain of their breakup all over again. But for some reason Scott needed to tell her something, and she would listen. She would listen because she still loved him.

"Well, Mom had sat me down a couple of days before she officially left Dad. She told me she wanted to talk to me about why she was thinking of leaving him and that...that she didn't want me to make any mistakes that might hurt me or...or you...later," he explained.

"Scott, it's...it's okay," Jacey stammered. "It's in the past. You really don't need to—"

"Yes. I do," Scott interrupted. "I...I want you to understand why...why I..."

"Why you left me?" she finished for him.

"Yes," he mumbled, casting a guilt-ridden glance to the floor. It was important to him. Jacey could see guilt heavy in his eyes, in the way his broad shoulders suddenly seemed to droop. For some reason he needed further closure, needed to tell her exactly why he'd broken up with her.

"Okay," Jacey said. "Go ahead." For a moment she felt seventeen again, felt the weight of loss, heartache, loneliness, fear, and overwhelming despair washing over her. If there was one thing Jacey had come to know over the past four years, it was that no woman ever got over being seventeen. Bodies changed and matured and aged, responsibility and experience demanded wiser decision-making and a different list of priorities, but all in all the heart of every woman on earth really never aged past seventeen. She knew Scott's retelling of their breakup would hurt just as much as the experience of it always had. Yet for his sake, she would endure it.

Scott drew in a deep breath and began again. "Mom was unhappy," he said. "I had known she was. Dad had known it. But I know now…it wasn't my fault… or Dad's. She had become selfish, though I didn't understand it really. She'd started into these feelings of having missed out because she got married so young. You know…never really dated anybody but Dad. You probably remember how she changed that year before she left."

Jacey nodded, thinking back on Mrs. Pendleton. It seemed to Jacey that Mrs. Pendleton, once so caring and nurturing, so pleasant and kind, had turned into her own evil twin the year before she'd left her family. She'd gone from wearing modest, pretty clothing to shopping at the stores in the mall where the rather rowdy crowd of teenagers shopped. She'd slowly begun to advertise her body, wear a ton of jewelry, and even had a floral bracelet tattooed around her right wrist. Yes, Jacey had noticed the change, but she'd been so involved in her own life, so incredibly in love with Mrs. Pendleton's handsome son, she hadn't really taken the time to consider it seriously.

"Well, she sat me down that day and told me she had too many regrets," Scott continued. "She'd never really had a steady boyfriend before my dad—'Been cheated out of my youth' is the way she'd put it. 'I got married at eighteen, right out of high school, and I didn't have a chance to have any fun before I did,' she said." Scott paused and released a heavy sigh before continuing, "She went on and on about how she'd been cheated, how she'd had me after only a couple of years of marriage, and how her whole life had become all about everybody but herself."

"But...but that's the point, isn't it?" Jacey said. "What would life be if all you worried about was yourself?"

Scott shrugged and said, "Miserable, I guess. At least to hear her tell it then. Though I think she's living proof of it now. What she's gone through since has really opened her eyes. At the time, however, all she could see was that she'd given up her life, her fun, everything she'd ever wanted to do or be. All she could see was she'd given it up for Dad and me."

Jacey frowned, more disgusted by Mrs. Pendleton's behavior than ever. She'd heard bits and pieces of how the woman's life had turned out. She'd had boyfriend after boyfriend, looking for fun and romance, love and excitement. It had taken her several years before she realized what a tragic mistake she'd made. Before she realized the kind of men she was keeping company with were losers, men who wanted to have a little fun for a few weeks and then move on. The last Jacey had heard, Charlotte Pendleton had somewhat realized the fatal error of her ways. Alone and unhappy, she was living in California working as a real estate agent.

"I was only nineteen, Jace," Scott said, his eyes

narrowed with the hurt of the memory. "I didn't have any experience, and…and she was my mom. I thought maybe she knew a little about life." He sighed and shook his head, continuing, "Anyway, she told me you'd have the same regrets…grow to resent me." Jacey frowned, furious at what she was hearing. "She told me you were even younger when we started dating than she was when she started dating my dad. She told me that she loved my dad when she was in high school as much as you loved me but that it was nothing more than a reason for you to resent me later. She said there would come a day when you'd wake up one morning and realize you'd missed out on your youth. You'd hate me for it and feel trapped, cheated, and desperate to escape." He shook his head and added, "You'd run from me like a caged lion. One day someone would leave the cage door open, and you'd see freedom on the other side and…and leave me…just like she was doing to Dad."

"No offense, Scott," Jacey angrily mumbled, "but your mother was a stupid, self-centered…idiot!" Instantly she realized what a hurtful thing she'd said and began to apologize. "I'm…I'm sorry. I…just…"

"No, no," Scott said, shaking his head. "You're right. She became just that…stupid and selfish. But at the time…I only knew Dad and I had ruined her life. And although it didn't take me too long to wise up, to realized what a load of sh—trash she'd fed me…she told me I'd ruin your life, and, well, I believed it long enough to ruin some things of my own. Didn't I?"

Jacey glanced away as he looked at her and smiled. His eyes were sad, filled with regret, and it caused her to want to reach out, throw her arms around his neck, and beg him to love her again.

"So…it was your mom," she said instead. At that moment, Jacey hated Charlotte Pendleton. Hated what she'd done to her husband and son, hated what she'd done to Jacey. And she did resent Scott for a moment—resented him for being too hurt himself, too gullible to know Jacey would never have had the regrets his mother did. She would never have wavered from loving him and loving life with him. "Your mom talked you into—"

"My mom…and…and your dad," Scott said.

"What?" Jacey exclaimed. "What do you mean 'my dad'?"

She watched as Scott swallowed hard, as if he were mustering up a profound amount of courage.

"I…I went to talk to you dad after…after my mom said what she did," he began to explain. "I didn't want to believe her, couldn't believe you would ever regret me. Still, the doubt was planted pretty dang firm in my mind, and so…so I went over to talk to your dad about it."

The hair on the back of Jacey's neck began to prickle, and she fought the urge toward fury. Surely her own father, knowing how entirely she'd loved Scott… surely he wouldn't have endeavored to strip him from her.

"I told him what my mom had said, and I asked

him for his thoughts, his opinion," Scott said. He looked to Jacey then, his eyes narrowing once more as he added, "He told me I should let you go. He told me I should let you have your youth, let you date other guys. Of course, he knew and knows you're nothing like my mom…but he did worry for you. He was worried because your life had become so singular to me."

"Please tell me you're making this up," Jacey whispered, though deep within she knew he was telling her the truth.

"He…he pointed out how you'd quit playing softball when I started playing football so you could go to my games…how you'd begun to stay home so much, never out with your girlfriends if I was busy and couldn't be with you," Scott said.

"I hated softball!" Jacey exclaimed.

"I know. But…but the doubt was already in my mind," he said.

"And…and I hardly had any girlfriends!" Jacey continued. "They all hated me because of…"

"Because of me," Scott finished for her. Again she saw a wave of guilt wash over him. "I know. I didn't get it then. Guys are so different. It's like that Rick Springfield song from the '80s…"Jessie's Girl." Sure, the guy singing the song was jealous…wanted his friend's girlfriend for himself. But…but he never did anything about it because Jessie was his friend. He just dealt with it. But girls…girls, on the other hand…they get mean and witchy, don't they?"

"That's beside the point, Scott," Jacey began to argue.

"Not to your dad," Scott said. "And he's your dad. He cares about you. He wants the best for you…just like he did then."

Jacey felt tears welling in her eyes as she asked, "Are you telling me that my dad…my dad told you to break up with me?"

"No," Scott said. "He just thought it would be good for me to give you some space. He…he didn't say it…but I think he worried you would have regrets one day. Oh, he knew you weren't like my mom, would never be like my mom. But…but he didn't want you to have any regrets."

"People have regrets no matter what they do, Scott," Jacey told him. "There are always regrets in life. Aren't there?" Her words were pointed, and Scott knew it.

He nodded. "Yep. There are," he said, looking to her. She knew what he meant. He regretted leaving her, and the knowledge helped a little. But only a little and he continued, "But my mom kind of hammered me about it over the next few days. I watched her leave Dad, watched her trying to act like she was eighteen again, and between her stupidity—and I loved her anyway—between her stuff and your Dad's advice, I…I started to wonder if…if I would ruin your life by keeping you."

"I wasn't a puppy, Scott," Jacey angrily countered, trying to hold back her tears.

"I know that," Scott said. "But I was young…

watching my family fall apart, trying to survive it. And so…so I…I did it. I set you free. I let you go because I didn't want to ruin your life." He exhaled a heavy sigh, as if an enormous burden had just been lifted and yet lingered.

Jacey was furious—furious with Scott's mother, furious with her own father. And furious with Scott! The day he'd broken her heart had been the worst day of her life. She knew there would probably never be another like it—for she certainly knew she would never love anyone, *could* never love anyone, the way she'd loved and still loved Scott. It was the deep remembered and lingering hurt in her, the anger over his revelation of what and who had contributed to her losing him, that drove her to act with such pure irrationality. Before Jacey could think clearly enough to calm herself, she'd faltered. In the next instant she lost control of her calm, rational mask.

"Don't you see, Scott…you ruined my life anyway!" she cried, suddenly bursting into tears. All at once, years of heartache overtook her, began wracking her body like a painful disease. Leaping to her feet, she pointed a trembling index finger at him and cried, "I…I haven't been able to love anybody else! I can't! No matter how hard I try…I can't! I compare every man I meet to you. Every time someone kisses me…I…I wish it were you!"

"Good!" Scott shouted, standing to meet her face-to-face, instantly unable to restrain his own anger. The hurt and fury in his own soul broiled in the ferocity of his eyes. Jacey gasped and then sobbed, startled by not only her own outburst but by his. "Good!" he repeated, reaching out and taking her chin firmly in one hand. Jacey could feel his hand trembling with rage and frustration, but he did not hurt her. Uncomfortable though his grip was, he did not hurt her. His voice broke with emotion as he lowered the volume of his speech and said, "Because I wanted it that way! I didn't want to let you go, Jacey. I didn't want to. I felt compelled to do it, and I wanted you to wish every man you ever knew from then on…I wanted you to wish it were me!"

Tears streamed down Jacey's face as she struggled to understand what he was telling her. Was he telling her he rejoiced in breaking her heart? In ruining her for any other man?

"I…I did not break up with you because I wanted it, Jacey!" he growled. His massive chest rose and fell with barely restrained fury. "If you don't know that by now…then…then…" he stammered, shaking his head. "I broke up with you because I thought it was the right thing to do…for *you*! Not for me, Jacey. Not once did I think it was the right thing for me! Your dad told me it wasn't fair to you. My…my mom told me you'd grow to resent me. I was young, confused… and you…you were even younger. So…I did it. I beat a cinderblock wall with my bare hand that day because I knew I was going to hurt you…because I thought I was going to die. And then I did it," he said, frowning.

A vision flashed through Jacey's mind—a memory of Scott's hand, knuckles bleeding, fingers swollen and purple. She hadn't really thought of it before, having only remembered her own heartache that day.

"I broke up with you and prayed," he growled. "I prayed for you to never get over me! I prayed for it…because I didn't want you to." He inhaled deeply, attempting to calm himself before adding, "And the irony of it all is…your dad, my mom…they were right in the end. Weren't they? In the end, if what you say is true…I ruined your life anyway."

Scott released her chin, clenched his teeth tightly, and drew in a deep breath. He was still furious. "I never got over you either, Jacey," he told her, pointing a shaking index finger at her as his eyes filled with moisture. "I never got over you…and I had the guilt to deal with on top of it all!" Jacey buried her face in her hands as he shouted and threw his powerful fist into the wall next to him. "Why, Jacey?" he shouted. "Why did you have to be so perfect? Why did you have to be so beautiful, so smart and funny?"

"I'm…I'm sorry," Jacey sobbed, uncertain as to what else to say and amazed at what she was hearing. He'd been hurt as deeply as she had. She'd always assumed since Scott did the breaking up he'd had an easier time of it. Jacey felt guilty for her accusations toward him. He hadn't ruined her life: she had ruined her life. He'd been nothing but a wonder of youth, a dream come true. If she hadn't been able to get over him, it wasn't his fault. She opened her mouth to tell him, but the words would not come.

Scott's chest rose and fell with barely restrained

fury. He put a hand to his head, running it firmly over his face and seeming to regain his senses. But Jacey looked up to him, puzzled when she heard him begin to laugh for a moment.

"I was a mess back then," he said, looking down at the floor. "You had me so twisted up I didn't know which way I was going half the time." Jacey frowned, wiping tears from eyes, trying to catch her breath as her sobbing began to even out. "The week before we broke up," he began. Jacey looked at him, and he shook his head and smiled at her—smiled as if he couldn't believe what he was saying. "The week before we broke up…I bought you a ring, Jace," he said.

"What…what do you mean?" Jacey asked. The past moments had been so charged with such a varying degree of emotion, she was having trouble keeping her wits about her.

"I bought you a damn ring," he repeated, shaking his head in disbelief. "Not an engagement ring… necessarily. But then again," he added, shrugging his shoulders, "what else would it have been for, huh?" He shook his head, ran his hand through his tousled hair, and said, "I bought you this little ring. It had three small diamonds on a gold band…and I had it engraved. 'Scott and Jacey—Past, Present, Future—Forever,' it said. You know, on the inside it said that." He seemed to be simmering down, but his revelation only caused Jacey's tears to begin anew. "I was going to go ahead and give it to you that day…but I didn't think it would matter to you then. It didn't seem right."

Jacey brushed the tears from her cheeks. "I…I do understand why you left me, Scott," she said in nearly a whisper. Looking up at him, she added, "I understand it now. But…but it doesn't make it any easier. It doesn't change the way I—"

"I know…I know," he said, nodding. "And…and I'm sorry, Jace. I really am sorry. I want you to believe that."

As a lone tear escaped one of Scott's eyes and trickled down his handsome cheek, more tears spilled over Jacey's. It was time to forgive him. She knew it with all her heart. As she'd carried such a miserable pain in her heart for so long, Scott had carried a miserable guilt, and now he needed to move on. Perhaps it was the reason he'd come; perhaps it was the reason he'd moved in so willingly with Harbine. Whatever the reason, Jacey knew it was time…time to let him go.

Jacey felt as if she might die, her stomach wrenched with such intense nausea and pain. She hoped she wouldn't lose control of it and throw up the way she had the day Scott had broken up with her four years before. She'd thrown up as soon as he'd left her sobbing in her bedroom, and for days she hadn't eaten, unable to hold anything down because of the horrible emotions wracking her body. But now—now she realized Scott had suffered as deeply as she had. Perhaps it was the guilt; perhaps he had loved her as much as she had loved him. Whichever it was, he needed her forgiveness, and so she gave it.

"I know you would never have hurt me…if you

could've avoided it, Scott," she told him. "I'm sorry I said such hateful, mean things to you. You…you don't deserve it."

Jacey looked up at him. Scott's eyes narrowed, his shoulders straightened, and she could see his jaw clenching.

"Tell me something, Jacey," he said. His voice was low, the residual anger in him apparent in his intonation. "Are you forgiving me because it's the right thing to do? Or do you really mean it?"

"I…I really…" Jacey began, puzzled at why he should doubt her and why it mattered.

He shook his head and held up a hand, a gesture that she should further consider her answer.

"Truly, Jace," he said. "I'm tired of doing the right thing. I'm so tired of saying what I should instead of what I want to. Of acting how I should instead of how I want to. And right now…I don't want to hear what you think the right thing to say is. I want to hear the truth. I want to know what you're really thinking."

Jacey glanced away for a moment. Her heart was pounding so hard within her it was causing her breastbone to ache. She loved Scott! She had never stopped, and she never would. For four years she'd still loved him. For four years she hadn't set eyes on him, and as he stood before her now, she loved him as much as she had the day he'd left her. She marveled at it, wondered how it could even be possible. Yet it was true, and more than anything at that moment she wanted him to know the truth. Before she forgave him and sent him into the arms of another woman, she wanted him to hear the truth one last time.

Brushing the tears from her cheeks once more, she drew in a deep breath and said, "I can truly forgive you, Scott," she began. "I already have. But…but I can never forget it…or you…or how I felt…how perfectly, how desperately I loved you. It will ache forever, and I will never, ever get over it." He turned his face from her a moment, and she nodded as she added, "You're right. It feels better…the truth…instead of trying to do what's exactly correct."

"Does it?" he asked, looking back to her, his eyes smoldering with emotion.

"Yes," she told him, for it was the truth. It felt better to tell him her true feelings rather than to let him off the hook with feigned complete forgiveness. It was selfish perhaps, but it was liberating in a manner too.

"Good," he said, reaching out and taking her face between his powerful hands, "because I'm sick to death of not saying what I really want to…of not doing what I really want to do."

Jacey gasped as Scott kissed her. His mouth was hot; his kiss was angry, powerful, driven. The moment his lips touched hers, Jacey was breathless, trembling. Every inch of her flesh tingled with a familiar pleasure—a pleasure that had been long absent.

Scott broke the kiss but continued to hold her face between his hands. His eyes narrowed as he said, "It was over a long time ago, Jacey. I know that. I…I can deal with it. I have dealt with it. But in these past four years, there hasn't been one moment that I've forgotten how beautiful you are, how warm your body feels in my arms…and I've never forgotten the way you taste. I want to taste you, Jacey…one more time. I want you one more time before you walk out of here and it's all finally over."

Jacey took hold of Scott's forearms, desperate for an anchoring support, afraid her knees would give way beneath her. Her heart ached cruelly, her stomach was sickened, her head pounded. She'd spent years trying to forget his kiss, trying to move beyond him. If he kissed her again now, it would mean the end of any possibility of doing either.

"Scott, I've tried so long to…if I…if I…"

"Quit thinking about what you should do, Jacey. For once do what you want to do," he whispered.

Jacey gazed into the fiery depth of his eyes. She studied his ruggedly handsome face, inhaled the scent of his oh-so-familiar cologne. He was all she had ever wanted. As far back as she could remember, Scott Pendleton was all she had ever wanted.

"Okay," Jacey breathed. Scott released the breath he'd been holding and drew her face toward his. He kissed her softly at first, playfully—the way he had so long ago—kissed the corner of her mouth, then her upper lip, then her lower lip. "Mouth, Scott. Mouth," Jacey softly whispered, the way she used to, long ago. The way she used to when she'd become impatient with his teasing, wanting nothing but the feel of his lips pressed to her own.

She felt him smile against her lips as he said, "Jace... do remember when you used to love me?"

"I do," she breathed. Oh, how she did remember, but her answer...her answer was twofold, for she still loved him. As desperately as ever she had, she still loved him.

A tear traveled over her cheek as Scott's mouth captured her own in a hot, zealous kiss. Instantly, their kiss exploded with passion! Years of maturing desire erupted. Years of unwanted separation, loss, heartache, and pain seemed to detonate as their impassioned exchange began to burn out of control.

Jacey couldn't breathe, and she didn't care! The taste of Scott's mouth, the feel of his five-o'-clock shadow on her cheeks, the sense of being held in his arms, safe against his powerful body, all combined to entirely bewitch her. She wanted nothing more than to remain in his arms, to savor his perfect kiss. Gathering her senses for a brief moment, Jacey marveled at how superbly Scott kissed. Certainly it was akin to the same kiss he'd owned as a boy but with the virile, wonton passion of a man added to enhance it!

Letting her fingers be lost in the softness of his hair, Jacey sighed as Scott paused their exchange to whisper, "Jacey...you know, don't you...you know I always wanted to be the one who—"

Jacey put her fingers to his lips to still his words. The growing desire and passion between them was already dangerous. This was to be their last kiss. Too many words and Jacey was uncertain as to how strong her resolve to resist begging him to love her, to never leave her again, could endure.

"I...I always wanted you to be the one, Scott," she whispered. Her confirmation seemed to be his undoing, and he took her mouth again with his own. His kiss was deeper, driven, nearly suffocating, and Jacey thought there would be no better way to die than to be smothered by Scott's kiss. And it was true, what she'd told him. She'd always dreamed, always wanted Scott Pendleton to be the man she married, to be the one she would entirely give herself to. More tears escaped her eyes, and her mind silently affirmed she still dreamt of it.

His hands were at her waist, gripping her shoulders, then lost in her hair. He caressed her face with the tips of his fingers, kissed her with a driven brutality one moment and playfully, gently, the next. He bound her in his arms, crushing her against the solid contours of his body, and Jacey received his kisses, responded to them, and implemented passiondriven kisses of her own—kissing him the way she'd wanted to for so very, very long.

She let her hands caress the breadth of his shoulders, frantically embraced him, let her fingertips caress the roughly shaven contours of his face. All the while her mind silently cried, *I love you, Scott! Please don't ever let go of me!*

"If...if I don't let you go now," he whispered,

kissing her neck lingeringly, "I might still be the one." Though she knew he was teasing, Jacey's heart leapt, her shattered dreams racing through her mind again. All her life she'd dreamt of one day marrying Scott, being Jacey Pendleton, and sleeping in his arms every night. Not so long ago she'd dreamt of having his children, kissing him every morning before making the bed they'd shared the night before. Her heart bled as she realized some other woman would now live her dreams, steal them away. Scott kissed her once more—kissed her softly, lingeringly, before taking her shoulders and holding her away from him.

It was over. After so long, so much heartache, so many dreams of Scott coming back into her life, Jacey knew it was over. She felt more alone than she ever had in her life. More frightened.

"Hold on a second, will you?" he said. Jacey nodded and watched as he disappeared into one of the bedrooms for a moment. Her entire body was trembling, weak. She felt as if she could close her eyes and drift into some odd unconsciousness. The taste of his mouth still lingered in hers; her flesh still sensed his touch. But it would all dissipate, she knew, and her memory of those moments would be only memories.

When he returned, he held his hand out to her and said, "I want you to have this. It was made for you. It's yours. I want you to have it…to know I meant everything I said to you when we were kids." Scott opened his hand, and Jacey saw the pretty ring lying in his palm. It was a gold band with a setting of three small diamonds. "It cost me a month's salary back then," Scott said. "But…it looks sorta cheap now."

"No," she whispered as her trembling fingers drew the ring from his palm. "It's beautiful." Another painful pang stabbed Jacey's heart as she saw the tiny inscription on the inside of the ring. "Scott and Jacey— Past, Present, Future—Forever," Jacey whispered as she read it out loud. She brushed more tears from her cheeks, astonished she even had enough moisture left in her body to produce them. "Thank you, Scott," she whispered, unable to look up at him. The ring was beautiful in its simplicity, beautiful in its once-loving meaning.

"I hope you'll wear it sometimes," he said. "You know…just for something pretty to have. All right… sexy angel?"

Jacey nodded, deeply wounded by his use of the familiar endearment. She slipped the ring onto her right ring finger, and, oh, how she wished she could wear it on the left! Oh, how desperately she wished Scott were still in love with her. How she wished she had the courage to try and make him fall in love with her again!

"Hey," he said then. "Thank you, Jacey…for pretending you've forgiven me."

Jacey nodded, brushed several more tears from her cheeks, and forced a smile. "You're welcome." Still dripping with tears, tired, and heartbroken, Jacey turned from him and started for the door.

"Hey, Jacey," Scott said, causing Jacey to turn and

look at him once more. She winced at the pain stabbing her heart as she gazed at him. "Um…see you around, huh?"

Jacey nodded and said, "See you around."

Once she'd left Scott's apartment, Jacey fled down the stairs and across the complex courtyard. Grateful Nora was still out with Harbine, Jacey threw herself on her bed and sobbed the bitter tears borne of a wound that would never heal. As she soaked her pillow with her tears, she glanced at the ring on her finger, wishing it could be a token of wonderment and undying love instead of a symbol of such a terrible loss.

After hours of tears and sobbing, Jacey found herself spent, empty of the moisture and energy needed to grieve further. She was aware of Nora entering the room somewhere deep in the night but could not awaken fully enough to greet her. And it was a good thing because she was too fully worn out to take the time to tell her dear friend about what had happened with Scott. It could wait…wait until morning…until Jacey's tears had replenished enough to be exhausted again.

CHAPTER FOUR

A week passed and then another—two weeks during which Jacey tried to begin recovering from seeing Scott again, from being held in his arms, from tasting his kiss again. Summer semester ended, autumn semester began, and Jacey tried to focus on her classes, tried not to burst into tears whenever she saw Scott in passing, either on campus or at the apartment complex.

"I can get on with my life now," Jacey had said to Nora the morning after Scott had kissed her, asked her forgiveness, and found his own closure.

"You liar!" Nora had exclaimed. "Don't let him just walk away, Jacey. Don't."

Yet Jacey didn't know what else to do. It had been obvious to her Scott had simply wanted to tell her why he'd broken up with her four years before. He'd wanted to tell her, hoped she would understand a little more and give him her forgiveness. And Jacey did forgive him. She did understand. Still, it didn't mean she could ever stop loving him. However, she decided to try. What other course was left to her?

Summer ended, and autumn began. And Jacey

tried not to cry herself to sleep every night but failed miserably.

♥

"Quit messing around, Jacey," Nora began one day as she sat at the kitchen table watching Jacey mix brownie batter. As usual, there were only two main subjects discussed between Nora and Jacey of late: Carl Harbine and Scott Pendleton. At the moment, the topic of conversation was Scott. "Win him back!" Nora demanded.

"He's finished, Nora," Jacey told her friend. "I've told you over and over and over again, and I don't know why you even keep bringing it up. He was finished a long time ago. He…he just had to purge his guilt, that's all. I've explained that to you a million times."

"That is such a crock, Jacey!" Nora said. "And I've explained that to *you* a million times! He never got over you any more than you ever got over him. And maybe…maybe that's the point."

"Have you seen him, Nora?" Jacey cried, tossing the spatula into the brownie batter with frustration. "Have you really, really gotten a good look at him? He's…he's gorgeous! He's perfect! He's funny and smart, heroic, and…and…over it!"

"You forgot totally buff," Nora added. "And he's not over it."

"He is over it, Nora. And," Jacey continued, gritting her teeth, "and I did not forget that he's totally buff. He walks around on campus, and girls are dropping dead at his feet. It's…it's just like high school. He's the boy every girl wants and—"

"And just like in high school, you're the one who should, and will, have him," Nora finished.

"It's different now, Nora…and you know it," Jacey said, picking up the spatula once more and scraping the sides of the bowl.

"Let's not wait for them to bake this time," Nora suggested. Going to the cupboard, she took down two cereal bowls. "Let's just eat the batter."

"Okay," Jacey said. More often than not, Nora and Jacey just ate the brownie batter instead of waiting for the mixture to bake. Sure, they considered the possibility of salmonella once or twice, but Nora always argued it was a type of food poisoning people usually survived. Jacey divided the batter into two bowls, and soon the two friends were sitting on the sofa enjoying a delicious treat.

"It's no different now, you know," Nora said, licking batter from her spoon.

"Yes, it is," Jacey said. "I told you. We talked about it. We…we had our last kiss. And this time…this time it's really over."

"Yeah, and what kind of a kiss was it, Jacey?" Nora asked. "A little peck on the cheek? I doubt it! I saw the whisker burn on your face that night. And your lips were so swollen it looked like you'd just had a bad collagen injection. Like I've been telling you—that, my darling, is not an 'it's really over' kiss. That's an 'I'm having trouble not whisking you to the bedroom' kiss."

"Nora!" Jacey exclaimed, but only because she felt obligated to.

"Don't 'Nora!' me, Jacey!" Nora said. "It's only over if you let it be. Let me show you something." Jacey watched as Nora set her brownie batter bowl down and began rummaging around in her purse. "Harbine gave these to me yesterday—prints of the pictures he took that first night he met Scott." Jacey licked her spoon as Nora flipped through the photos. "Here. Look at this one," she said, handing a particular photo to Jacey. "Remind you of anything you've seen before?"

Jacey took the photo, wincing at the piercing pain in her heart as she looked at the image of Scott. Jacey had forgotten Harbine had taken two photos of her and Scott together that night. The first had been posed, Scott's arm around Jacey's shoulders. Jacey remembered it because his touch had been so heavenly. It was the second photo, however, that Nora pointed to again— the one Harbine had snapped as Jacey had held her hand out to receive his camera in order to take a photo of Scott and Harbine together. Jacey studied the photo. She was looking at the camera, her hand outstretched toward Harbine because he had just asked her to take photos of him and Scott. Scott, however, was looking at Jacey. Jacey's heart leapt. Scott wore the same expression he'd worn in Nora's favorite photo of Scott and Jacey in the past—the one taken at the lake when she'd been making a face and wearing the ugly purple bathing suit. As Jacey had been looking at Harbine, holding her hand out toward him, Scott had been looking at Jacey, grinning at her the way he had in the older photo.

"It's that same expression on his face, Jacey," Nora said. "It's the same way he was looking at you in that old picture at the lake." Nora took a bite of batter, savoring it before adding, "Nothing's changed, Jacey. You guys just…just got derailed, that's all. You just have to get back on the track."

"I didn't have the courage to pursue him back then, Nora. He made the first move. How can you possibly think I can find the courage now?" Jacey said. For a moment, her heart had taken flight, hopeful Nora was correct in her assumption of Scott's still loving Jacey.

"He made the first move this time too, Jacey," Nora said. "Can't you see that? He literally made the first move. He moved here!"

Jacey shook her head and handed the photo back to Nora. "He's moving, all right. He's moving on, Nora."

"He hasn't had time to move on yet, Jacey," Nora told her. "Don't let fear stop you from going for it! I mean, in reality, can it be any worse than it already is?"

Nora was right. Jacey's heart was already splintered into so many pieces it would take forever to puzzle it back together. Still, Scott wouldn't have made such a big effort to "end" things if he hadn't really wanted things ended.

"Oh, I know!" Nora exclaimed, suddenly clapping her hands together, kicking her feet, and giggling excitedly. "Buy him!"

"What?" Jacey asked, completely confused at her roommate's behavior and suggestion.

"Buy him!" Nora said again. "Harbine signed Scott up for the Indentured Servant Sale...you know, for the guys' half of the week. You could buy him! That would let him know you were still interested, *and* you could have your way with him for three whole days."

"He's signed up?" Jacey asked, mortified. The thought of Scott being up for grabs made her nauseated.

"Yep! Harbine signed him up," Nora said. "I guess he wasn't too thrilled, but then Harbine explained it was for charity and stuff. You have to buy him, Jacey! It'll send the message you still want him."

"I...I couldn't do that," Jacey stammered. "What if he was disappointed? What if it upset him?"

"You are such a chicken, Jacey!" Nora exclaimed. "Just go for it! What do you have to lose?"

"He'll draw a mint, Nora," Jacey said. "Remember? Guy Parker went for eight hundred bucks last year!"

"Well? How much cash do you have?" Nora asked.

"About four hundred," Jacey answered as the idea of buying Scott at the Indentured Servant Sale began to settle in her mind.

"I've got a grand in my savings. I'll lend it to you," Nora offered. Jacey couldn't help but smile at her friend's enthusiasm. It was a good idea. And Nora was right—what did Jacey have to lose that she hadn't already lost once?

"Okay," Jacey agreed. "I'll...I'll do it, Nora. I will."

"Good!" Nora said, taking a bite of her batter. "You won't regret it."

Jacey frowned for a moment, however. "But…what if someone pays off his debt?"

The system of the Indentured Servant Sale included a clause enabling a bidder to pay off the indentured servant's imaginary debt. For two thousand dollars, a prospective bidder could pay off the candidate's debt before the sale and acquire the person they wanted before the bidding even began.

"Right!" Nora said. "Like anybody has that kind of money to blow on this thing. I've heard it's only happened once before."

"Yeah…to Guy Parker…his freshman year," Jacey reminded Nora.

"No one in this complex has that kind of cash, Jacey," Nora told her. "Don't worry. We've got fourteen hundred big ones between us. We'll get him."

"But…but then you can't buy Harbine," Jacey said.

"I'll get Harbine for a steal, Jacey," Nora giggled. "No one would dare to outbid me for my own man."

There was a knock on the door, and Nora and Jacey simultaneously called, "Come in."

Jacey gasped slightly, however, when Scott opened the door and stepped into the apartment. She was angry at the fact she couldn't even look at him without her heart racing and excess moisture flooding her mouth. He was wearing an old white T-shirt that had the sleeves torn away and a pair of red board shorts. He looked delicious!

"Hey, Scott," Nora greeted. "What's up?"

"We're out of dish soap, and the kitchen is raunchy. You ladies have any I can borrow? I didn't want to have to run all the way to the store," he explained.

"Sure," Nora said, nudging Jacey with one elbow.

"Y-yeah. We have dish soap," Jacey managed.

Scott frowned and walked to where the two girls sat on the sofa. "What are you two eating?" he asked.

"Brownie batter," Jacey said, holding her bowl up for him to inspect.

He chuckled and asked, "Batter?"

"Yeah," Jacey said. "It's better when it's not baked."

"Let me try," Scott said, opening his mouth in a gesture Jacey should feed him a bite of the batter. Jacey's eyes widened, and she tried to keep her hand from trembling too noticeably as she spooned a glob of batter into his mouth. Scott took hold of her wrist as she began to withdraw the spoon from his mouth, licking the spoon thoroughly and mumbling, "Mmm! It is better." For a moment his eyes locked with her own, and Jacey feared she might leap to her feet and throw herself against him, begging for his love.

"I'll get you some dish soap," Nora said, giggling quietly as she stood up.

"Oh my heck!" Megan exclaimed as she entered by way of the open front door. "Fancy meeting you here, Scott."

Jacey frowned as Scott closed his eyes for a moment, sighing. Turning to face Megan, he said, "Yeah...fancy that."

The hair on the back of Jacey's neck prickled. Something was happening she wouldn't like. "He…he came to borrow dish soap," Jacey stammered, wondering why she even endeavored to offer an explanation.

"Whew!" Megan breathed, raising her eyebrows. "There for a moment I was afraid he'd come just to see you…and that would never do when we have a date planned for tonight. Would it, Scott?"

"I guess not," Scott muttered, glancing back to Jacey. There was a rather unhappy, somewhat daring expression in his eyes, and Jacey did not know what to make of it.

"Here's your soap, Scott," Nora said. "Oh. Hi, Meg."

"Scott and Megan are going out tonight, Nora," Jacey said, standing and heading for the kitchen. Tears were already stinging her eyes, her heart already pounding with furious jealousy and hurt.

"Hey, Jace," Scott said, taking hold of her arm and stopping her escape for a moment.

Jacey forced a smile at him and said, "Don't worry about bringing the dish soap back, Scott. We have an extra bottle under the sink." She couldn't stop her eyes from lingering on his mouth for a moment, couldn't stop the moisture and desire for his kiss gathering in her own.

"You're going out with Scott?" Nora asked Megan. Jacey shook her head at her roommate, silently begging her not to give Megan any clues about how Jacey might be feeling.

"Yep!" Megan proudly announced. "It took some coaxing…but he finally agreed."

It did make the tiniest speck of a difference to Jacey—the fact Megan had obviously asked Scott out instead of the other way around. Still, she had no desire to be in the presence of a woman who was pursuing the man she still so violently loved.

"Well, I've gotta get ready for class," Jacey said, slowly pulling her arm out of Scott's grasp. "See you guys later."

Walking quickly to her room, she shut the door and let the tears escape her eyes. She clutched at the pain in her bosom, knowing there would be no soothing it. Having Scott near was going to be unbearable. Watching him date other girls would no doubt kill her. Nora was right. She had to buy him at the servant sale. She had to let him know she wanted him.

"What a hoochie!" Nora said, bursting into the bedroom. "Megan! I've always known she was hooch!" Nora took Jacey by the shoulders, forcing her to look at her. "Suck it up, Jacey! Buy him at that stupid sale, and let him know how you feel. He doesn't want to go out with Megan. He still wants you."

"I don't know if I can take this, Nora!" Jacey said. "I can't…I can't know he's with her tonight…wonder what they're doing…"

"That's why we're staking it out," Nora said. "We'll keep an eye on them…make sure Megan doesn't lay a hand on your man."

Jacey smiled through her tears, delighted by Nora's

sneaky brain. A tiny glimmer of hope had begun to smolder in Jacey's soul. It was small…but it was there.

♥

"Megan is such an idiot," Nora whispered as she and Jacey sat in the balcony of the old movie theater. The balcony was not only the perfect place from which to spy on Megan and Scott sitting in the theater seats below, but it was also great cover for espionage. "I mean," Nora continued, "does she really think he's going to fall for the 'let's snuggle in the theater' thing?"

Jacey didn't smile. Her attention was too fixated on the couple sitting below them. Megan indeed had grand designs on Scott. It had been obvious throughout the entire course of the evening. It was obvious in the way she flirted with him, always had to be touching him in some manner. And Scott, though ever polite, did not appear to return her interest in any regard. Still, Jacey found herself praying for their evening together to end. She worried about the good night moment—the moment when Scott would leave Megan at her apartment door. Would he kiss her good night? If not out of desire, out of obligation? Jacey was certain she could not endure it, but she had to know.

"Finally! They're leaving," Nora said. "Come on. It's late. He's got to take her home now."

Fifteen minutes later, Nora and Jacey were hiding behind a large shrub in the apartment complex courtyard watching as Scott walked Megan to her door.

"Oh, Scott," Megan sighed, smiling, "I had such a great time tonight."

"I'm glad," Scott said.

"You're such a gentleman," Megan told him. "It's been ages since I've been out with a man who opened doors for me."

Jacey looked at Nora, who rolled her eyes and whispered, "That's all she's got? Give me a break." But Jacey's heart began to pound with anxiety as she watched Megan take hold of the front of Scott's shirt.

"I think I could really, really like you, Scott Pendleton," Megan said as she raised herself on her tiptoes, obviously intending to kiss Scott good night.

"Nora!" Jacey gasped, mortified at what was about to transpire before her. Scott, though not initiating the kiss himself, did not turn from Megan or make to evade her actions.

"Eat dirt and die, Megan!" Nora whispered as she picked up a pebble from the ground and sent it hurtling toward the couple.

"Ow!" Megan shouted, releasing Scott's shirt and doubling over in pain. One hand went to her forehead, and she began rubbing the tender area.

"You okay?" Scott asked.

Jacey's mouth hung open in astonishment as Nora simply mumbled, "Take that, you hoochie."

"I'm fine," Megan said. "Something just hit me in the head. It really hurt."

"You're bleeding," Scott said after examining her forehead. "You better get inside and take care of that."

"I…I guess so," Megan stammered. The moment was lost, and she knew it. "I'll see you tomorrow?"

"Yeah," Scott said as he waved at her and sauntered off into the darkness.

Megan stood outside a moment longer, looking around as if expecting to see some would-be assailant.

Once she'd gone inside, Nora giggled. "That felt good!"

Jacey smiled and whispered, "You are so bad!"

"And aren't you glad?"

"Boo!"

Jacey and Nora both let out a startled scream as Harbine suddenly poked his head through the shrub and said, "What are you guys up to?"

"Harbine!" Nora exclaimed, slapping him softly on the cheek. "You scared the snot out of us!"

Harbine chuckled and pushed his way through the shrub, sitting down between the two girls.

"You guys were spying on Scott, weren't you?" he chuckled. "Dudes...you are so busted!"

"Now don't you go saying anything, Carl!" Nora said, shaking a warning index finger at him. "Don't you whisper a word!"

"Whatever," Harbine said, rolling his eyes.

"Harbine...you can't tell," Jacey pleaded. "Please."

"Jacey," Harbine began, dramatically placing a hand over his heart, "dude...do you think I would betray you? Don't you think I can keep a secret?"

Jacey smiled, delighted, as she studied Harbine from head to toe. The adorable, sloppy young man was just too loveable. She knew he could be trusted.

"And besides," he continued, "if you're worried about Megan…don't be."

"What do you mean?" Nora asked. Jacey was suspicious that—no—Jacey was certain Harbine and Nora spent a lot of time talking about the "Scott and Jacey" situation. Therefore, she wondered why Nora seemed to be as surprised as she did at Harbine's instructions.

"Scott only went out with Megan 'cause she's been asking him, like, three times an hour, sixteen hours a day," he explained. "She bugs him. That's all."

"A lot of guys who bug me ask me out…and I don't go," Jacey said.

"Jacey, Jacey, Jacey," Harbine said, shaking his head and taking Jacey's hands in his own. "I'm Scott's roommate, dude. We're tight. We share stuff. So don't ask me to tell you stuff he wouldn't want me to."

"Did I?" Jacey asked, confused.

"Okay. I'll cave on one thing," Harbine said. Nora giggled, delighted with her boyfriend's eccentric ways. "The other day…I can tell you this because he doesn't know I know it, and therefore, it's not a secret…right?"

"Right!" Nora confirmed, nodding at him, urging him to continue.

"Totally," Harbine said, nodding in response. "So," he continued, lowering his voice and looking straight into Jacey's eyes, as if he were about to reveal the secret of all secrets, "the other day, he's online, like, ordering underwear or something." Jacey couldn't help but smile at Harbine's serious expression. It was so uncharacteristic. "So…he's, like, ready to order—boxer-briefs, in case you're wondering. So he's ready to order, right…and he doesn't have his wallet. So he asked me to go to the bedroom and get his debit card out of his wallet for him. So…I'm in there, right…and I'm looking for his debit card…and guess what?"

Harbine paused. Nora rolled her eyes with impatience and said, "What, Carl? What?"

Harbine's eyes narrowed, and he lowered his voice. "I saw his photo thing. You know…that thing in your wallet where you keep photos?"

"Yeah," Nora urged.

"Well," Harbine continued, "there was only one photo in there…and guess whose it was?"

Jacey felt delight begin to well in her bosom as Harbine nodded and whispered, "Miss Jacey Whittaker…that's who."

"Really?" Jacey couldn't help but exclaim.

Harbine nodded and said, "Yep. Dude…you were younger and wearing, like, a pink sweater. Your hair was a little different…but it was you."

"A pink sweater with little white stripes?" Jacey asked.

"Totally, dude!" Harbine confirmed.

"It was my junior year picture," Jacey whispered, looking to Nora.

"It was the only photo in his wallet, dude," Harbine said, nodding. "The only one."

"Jacey!" Nora exclaimed then. "Quit messing around and go for it!"

"You should definitely quit messing around, dude," Harbine said, nodding in agreement.

"What are you guys doing back there?"

Jacey and Nora gasped. Even Harbine gasped, startled as Scott suddenly stepped behind the shrub to join them.

"Dude," Harbine said, standing up and bumping knuckles with Scott, their established greeting. "The girls are looking for night crawlers."

Jacey wanted to sink into the ground and squirm away with any night crawlers inhabiting the soil beneath the shrub. Harbine was adorable, smart, funny, witty, and so very, very random.

"Night crawlers?" Scott asked, frowning as his eyes met Jacey's. Instantly, the familiar aching throb began in Jacey's chest.

"Um…yeah," Nora said, rising to her feet and dusting off her knees. "We're um…um…"

"We're wanting to…to plant some…some ivy in a pot in our apartment…and we thought if we put some worms in the pot too…they might help it to…to…" Jacey stammered.

"To flourish!" Harbine finished, proudly winking at Nora. Nora shook her head and smiled lovingly at her boyfriend.

"Oh," Scott said, appearing unconvinced. "Any luck?"

"Unfortunately not," Nora said, standing and brushing off the seat of her pants.

"How was your date with Megan, dude?" Harbine

asked. Jacey glanced away quickly, uncomfortable as Scott's eyes fell to her.

Scott shrugged and said, "Okay, I guess."

Jacey couldn't help herself; she had to look at him. As she did, however, she immediately wished she hadn't, for a longing began in her so thoroughly painful it caused her to hold her breath for a moment.

"Well," Nora said then, "I guess we better be getting in. It's late."

"Yeah," Harbine said, leaning forward and kissing Nora sweetly on the mouth. "I've got early classes tomorrow."

"Good night," Nora said to Harbine. "See you later, Scott."

"See you," Scott said, nodding at her. "Good night, Jace," he said to Jacey then.

Jacey forced a friendly grin and said, "Good night, Scott." Oh, how she wished he would pull her into his arms and kiss her! Oh, how desperately she wished she would never have to leave him, could stay in his arms forever!

Scott turned to leave but exclaimed, "Oh! I almost forgot." He reached into the back pocket of his jeans and withdrew his wallet. "I found something for you, Jace. I've been carrying it around for a couple of days… just a stupid thing I thought you might like for your autumn scrapbook." He pulled something out of his wallet and frowned for a moment, asking, "Do you still do it? That notebook you used to put pumpkin pictures and things in?"

Jacey smiled and tried to breathe normally. How delightful he would remember her autumn scrapbook! How fabulous he would still think to give her something for it.

"Yeah, I still add to it," Jacey admitted. She glanced at Nora to see her smiling an *I told you so* smile.

"Good. Here," Scott said, handing her a torn strip of paper. "I saw it in a parenting magazine when I was at the dentist last week."

Jacey felt her eyebrows raise, her smile broaden. "A parenting magazine?" she couldn't help but giggle.

"Yeah," he admitted. "Some other dude was hogging the only sports magazine in the office. Don't laugh. There was a great article on colicky babies in there too."

"Dude," Harbine said, "you are way too easily entertained."

Jacey bit her lip, trying to stifle the delighted giggle threatening to erupt from her throat. How adorable! The very image of Scott sitting in the dentist's office flipping through a parenting magazine was too adorable.

"Shut up, dude," Scott told Harbine. Then, pointing to the strip of paper Jacey held, he said, "Check it out. It's totally you."

Still smiling, Jacey looked down at the paper and read aloud, "*Far the fields of pumpkin roll, up over Harvest's golden knoll. In all of this October's bliss is lovely Autumn's giving kiss.*"

Jacey smiled and looked up to Scott with a delighted sigh.

Scott smiled, nodded his head, and said, "Nice, isn't it?"

"Very nice," Jacey told him. "Thank you, Scott."

"Anytime, babe," he said, winking at her.

Instantly Jacey's smile faded. Once again he stood before her as the tangible example of what was yet intangible. "We'll...we'll see you guys later," Jacey stammered, turning and walking away.

"Good night, guys," she heard Nora echo. A moment later, Nora fell into step beside her.

"Oooo! That was telling!" Nora whispered.

"That was...was thoughtful," Jacey said. In truth, Scott's thoughtfulness and the tone of the quote he'd given her...hope had begun to bloom in her bosom again. Jacey worried, knowing hope was dangerous where Scott was concerned. She wondered if she'd really have the courage to bid on him at the Indentured Servant Sale. The sale was in five days. She'd have to spend every moment struggling to be brave—brave and confident. Yet she looked down at the piece of paper, a tiny quote torn from the page of a dentist's office magazine. Surely he'd been thinking of her, enough to notice the quote. Maybe she could buy him at the sale. Maybe he would even like being bought by her.

"It's a quote," Jacey said, not wanting to reveal too much of her hopes even to Nora.

"It's a quote about kissing!" Nora reminded her.

"He was thinking about kissing you when he read it. No doubt about it."

Jacey's smile faded as she remembered the moment when Megan had almost succeeded at kissing Scott good night.

"In my dreams," Jacey mumbled.

"Your dreams have come true before," Nora said, taking Jacey's hand. "Come on! Let's get our jammies on, slip into our beds, and talk about our favorite kissing moments!"

Jacey couldn't help but smile. Nora's delight was infectious.

"Okay!" she agreed, bursting into giggles as they dashed for the apartment.

♥

Hours later, Jacey lay in bed attempting to drift off to sleep. Sleep was elusive, however, for all she could think about was mustering the courage to bid on Scott at the servant sale. She was frightened. Would he be upset? Would he be glad? What would she do with him if she did manage to outbid everyone else and win? Eventually sleep came, and just before it did, Jacey smiled, imagining Scott sitting in a dentist's office reading a parenting magazine—an article about colicky babies.

"That's adorable," Jacey whispered, smiling as she drifted to sleep…into dreams of kisses with Scott in cool autumn breezes.

CHAPTER FIVE

Jacey watched, smiling and clapping with the crowd as Nora walked up onto the makeshift stage. Jacey laughed as Nora snapped a plastic shackle onto Harbine's ankle, placing the accompanying plastic ball and chain attached to it on the floor beside his foot.

"Thank you, Nora," Carla began, "for your generous contribution in purchasing Carl's indentured servitude." Carla smiled and turned toward Harbine. "Carl Harbine," she announced, "having sold yourself into servitude for a period not to exceed, but no less than, three days and three nights…you must agree to do your master's—in this case, mistress's—bidding. Each and every task asked of you."

"I agree," Harbine said, per tradition.

"Then Nora…enjoy your man! Carl Harbine and Nora Whitman, ladies and gentlemen!"

Everyone whistled, laughing and applauding as Nora took hold of Harbine's hand and led him from the stage. Jacey shook her head and giggled as they came to stand beside her.

"Too cute, Nora…the ball and chain," Jacey said.

"Yeah, Nora," Harbine said, smiling. "Pretty clever. But...but what are you going to make me wear?" he asked.

Half the fun of the Indentured Servant Sale was seeing the outlandish clothes and costumes the winning bidders had their indentured servants wear. Just as Jacey had to dress in the ridiculous French maid's costume the previous fall, now she was as impatient as Harbine was to see what Nora would want him to wear.

Nora reached down and picked up the small duffle bag sitting at Jacey's feet. Handing it to Harbine, she smiled, giggled, and said, "Here you go, muffin! They've set up a dressing booth behind the stage. Get to it!"

Harbine raised his eyebrows and shook his head at Jacey, saying, "Dude...I don't like that smile on her face."

"Payback, Harbine," Jacey told him. "Don't expect any sympathy from me...*monsieur*."

"Touché, twerp," Harbine said. Then he smiled, took a deep breath, and headed for the dressing booth. Jacey and Nora both giggled as they watched him walk away, the plastic ball and chain bouncing along behind him.

A few minutes later, Jacey clamped her hand over her mouth to soften the ripples of laughter wracking her body when Carl Harbine appeared from behind the stage dressed from head to shackled ball-and-chained ankle...as a pirate! Nora squealed with delight, throwing her arms around Harbine's neck and kissing him square on the mouth. Oddly enough, Harbine looked surprisingly perfect as a pirate. From his bandana-covered head, blousy white shirt, and long red coat to his black pants and knee-high boots! Everyone applauded, drawing amusement from Harbine's transformation.

"Ladies and gentlemen," Carla announced via the microphone at her podium on the stage, "I give you the dread pirate Harbine!"

"A pirate, Nora?" Harbine chuckled. "Blimey!"

"I love it! I love it! I knew I would!" Nora exclaimed, rubbing her hands together with excitement.

"Next up on this afternoon's agenda," Carla began, "Scott Pendleton!" The crowd erupted into cheering and catcalls—especially the girls. Instantly Jacey's confidence and courage began to wane. Every girl in the crowd, every girl who hadn't already bid and bought a boy, readied their numbered ping-pong paddles serving as bidding paddles.

"What if fourteen hundred isn't enough?" Jacey whispered to Nora.

"It will be," Nora said, but Jacey knew Nora was as worried as she was.

"Don't worry, lassies," Harbine said, looking about and raising his brow in astonishment. "I've got three hundred under my bed in my shoe. We'll get him."

But Jacey was not so convinced. She knew there weren't many girls in the apartment complex who could afford to pay college expenses and two thousand dollars to blow on such a thing as prepurchasing a guy at the sale. Still, there were a few. Jacey's innards began to tremble. She might not win him, and then what? Then she'd have to watch another girl "have her way with" him for three days!

"Okay, ladies. Settle down now," Carla said. "Settle down." The crowd quieted a moment, but when Scott stepped from behind the stage curtain and into full view, the whistling, cheering, and applauding began again.

"Ladies! Ladies, please!" Carla said, striking her gavel on the podium several times before the crowd quieted again. Jacey looked to Scott, sympathy for him washing over her as she saw the color drain from his face.

"Maybe…maybe I shouldn't have made him do this," Harbine mumbled.

Nora looked to her boyfriend, rolling her eyes with exasperation and saying, "You think?"

"Yeah," Harbine said. "The dude looks a little… disconcerted."

"You're too much, babe," Nora said, taking Harbine's hand in her own as she gazed adoringly at him.

But Jacey had no time to feel happy for her friends. Her stomach was in knots, and as Scott looked at her and tried to force a smile, she felt all the more desperate to win him…for his sake as well as hers.

"Okay," Carla began, "let's start the bidding at…" Carla paused as another girl assisting her appeared from behind the stage curtain. Cupping one hand at Carla's ear, the girl must have whispered something astonishing—for Carla's eyes widened.

"Are you serious?" Carla said, loud enough for the microphone to pick up her voice. The girl assisting her nodded, and Carla muttered, "Well…I'm not too surprised."

Jacey looked to Scott, who wore an expression of wanting to bolt and run. He nervously straightened his shoulders and released a heavy sigh.

"Well, ladies and gentlemen," Carla began again, "it looks like we have a payoff!"

"What?" Nora exclaimed.

"Oh, no!" Harbine groaned, putting a hand over his eyes for a moment.

Jacey felt ill, close to vomiting, as the contents of her stomach churned. It was exactly what she had feared. Some stupid girl had anteed up two grand to make certain she got to spend three days in Scott's exclusive company. Jacey was able, somehow, to keep her tears in check, but her stomach was another matter. She put a hand over her mouth for a moment, endeavoring to calm herself.

She watched as Scott's jaw tightened as he looked to Harbine. Harbine shook his head in disbelief and shrugged his shoulders.

"Scott Pendleton," Carla began, "your debt has been paid in full. Therefore, having sold yourself into servitude for a period not to exceed, but no less than, three days and three nights…you must agree to do your master's—in this case, mistress's—bidding. Each and every task asked of you."

Scott said nothing, simply nodded, his jaw still angrily clenched.

"Then Megan Tannis…annoy…I mean, enjoy your man," Carla announced, with a lack of enthusiasm. Megan squealed and bounded up onto the stage, throwing her arms around Scott's neck. He smiled a rather forced-looking smile and returned her embrace, although loosely. "Scott Pendleton and Megan Tannis, ladies and gentlemen."

The crowd whistled and applauded once more. Jacey feared she might lose control of her senses and begin screaming, rushing to Megan, and tearing her hair out with her bare hands. Megan took Scott's hand and led him from the stage. After squealing and excitedly hopping around for a few moments, she handed Scott a duffle bag and pointed to the dressing booth.

Jacey watched as Scott walked to where she stood with Nora and Harbine on his way to the booth.

Pausing for a moment as he reached them, he shook his head slightly at Harbine and through clenched teeth almost growled, "You're a dead man, bro."

"Dude," Harbine whispered, shaking his head, still stunned with disbelief, "I had no idea Megan had that kind of dough."

Scott drew in a deep breath. It was obvious he was irritated with his friend and at the same time understood it was out of Harbine's hands. Granting Harbine a forgiving nod, he looked at Jacey for a moment.

"It's okay. Right?" he said with a wink of encouragement.

What could Jacey say or do? It was obvious Scott was experiencing great trepidation about the entire matter. Still, he'd committed to be involved in the sale, and it was always a risk. That was part of the fun. Wasn't it?

Unable to do anything else but fight to keep from vomiting, Jacey shrugged her shoulders and then nodded. Scott nodded again and inhaled deeply as he headed for the dressing booth.

A few minutes later, Scott stepped from behind the stage dressed as perfectly akin to a Hollywood cowboy as anyone Jacey had ever seen. The crowd erupted into catcalls, whistles, and applause, but Jacey could only stare at him, her mouth gaping open in astonishment.

A weathered cowboy hat on his head, he wore a black front-panel shirt, strategically tattered blue jeans, and a banged-up pair of black cowboy boots.

"Ma'am," he said, touching the brim of his hat as he passed Jacey. Oddly, Jacey felt a delighted thrill shudder through her being at the sight of him in such attire. He was a perfect and very handsome cowboy! No doubt Megan had pulled the idea from her dreams.

Scott looked at Harbine and under his breath muttered, "When I hang you, I'm gonna hang you high, man." Shaking his head, he headed toward the center of the crowd to meet Megan.

"Perfect!" Megan squealed.

"Ladies and gentlemen," Carla announced from the pulpit, "I give you everybody's favorite ranch hand... Scott Pendleton!"

Everyone clapped and shouted, but Jacey knew if she lingered, the contents of her stomach would end up all over Harbine and Nora.

"Time to go," Jacey said, turning and trying to slowly and casually exit the crowd in the courtyard.

"You okay, Jacey?" Harbine asked once the threesome was safely back to Nora and Jacey's apartment.

"I'm fine," Jacey lied.

"I'm sorry, Jacey," Harbine began, kneeling down in front of her as she sank into the sofa. "I...I just didn't think anybody here this year had that kind of money."

"It's not your fault, Harbine," Jacey said. It was painfully obvious Harbine was aware of the depth of Jacey's feelings for Scott. Whether from information offered by Nora or his own observations, Harbine knew Jacey still loved the boy of her dreams.

"This is ridiculous!" Nora exclaimed. "You march out there and rip him out of Megan's arms! And I'll tell you this...she ain't never invited over here for pancake night anymore!"

"It's not Megan's fault," Jacey said, even though her flesh burned with jealousy. "She doesn't know that I—"

"Quit acting like such a saint, Jacey!" Nora told her. "Walk out there, throw your arms around his neck, kiss him hard on the mouth, and get on with it! All this pussyfooting around is driving me crazy!"

"Nora, it's not that simple, and you know—" Jacey began.

"Sure it is!" Nora exclaimed. "Watch." Nora took

hold of Harbine's coat lapels and urged him to his feet. "I love you, Scott Pendleton! Blow off Megan, the pancake-pinching hoochie, and come to me!" she said. Nora then pulled Harbine against her, kissing him hard on the mouth.

"Nice!" Harbine chuckled, smiling down at Nora as she released his pirate lapels.

Jacey wished she had the courage to tell Scott she was still in love with him, to go to Megan and tell her she'd have to get a refund for her "purchase." But the problem was twofold. First, Scott seemed so unobtainable, so intimidating. How could she go to such a man as he'd become, confess her undying, unending, never-got-over-you love? Second, the truth of it was Scott had broken Jacey's heart. Truly, completely, and irrevocably broken her heart. After four years she'd still been unable to completely recover, to fall in love with anyone else. And when Scott had walked back into her life, Jacey had known she never would. Courage to tell him aside, Jacey knew she could not bear losing him again. If a miracle were possible and Scott could, for some miraculous reason, love Jacey again, the thought of trying to endure losing him again was unfathomable. Fear. In the end, it boiled down to plain and simple fear. Fear of rejection—fear of losing the magnificent person Jacey had always loved more than anything.

Harbine looked to Jacey, nodding with understanding. "Don't be scared of him, Jacey," he said. "There ain't nothing to be scared of with Scott."

Jacey smiled at Harbine, stood, and hugged the scruffy pirate.

"Thanks, Harbine," she told him. "But you see...I already know different." Brushing a tear from her cheek, she added, "You two go on and have fun. I'll be fine. It's a silly thing for me to be upset about. Really it is. What could happen between them in only three days?"

Jacey tried to push the memory of Harbine and Nora enjoying their first passionate kiss only four days after Harbine had purchased Jacey at last year's Indentured Servant Sale. She tried to forget Carla's sister getting engaged the previous spring to a guy she'd only known for two weeks. Surely Megan wasn't Scott's type. Jacey was his type! At least, she had been once upon a time. Surely his taste hadn't changed so dramatically as to fall for a ditz like Megan. Surely, after four years found Scott still unattached, surely three days wouldn't make a difference. Would it?

Still, later that evening as Jacey looked out the window of her darkened apartment to the dancing couples in the courtyard, she doubted her rather arrogant knowledge of Scott's character. Nora was dancing with the dread pirate Harbine, just as every other girl was in the arms of her "servant," the wares from the day's charity sale. Seething jealousy and anger caused Jacey's breathing to become more rapid as she watched Scott holding Megan as they danced. One hand at her waist, the other holding hers in dance position, Jacey was at least slightly grateful Scott wasn't holding Megan tightly against his body. Yet as he smiled at something Megan said, chuckled, and said something back, Jacey was furious. She wanted to scream! To run away home and leave all the frustration and fear behind. Suddenly she wished she were just nine or ten again when life was carefree and full of dreams…before it had turned difficult and full of doubt and heartbreak.

Jacey gasped as Scott glanced over toward the apartment. She ducked below the window, hoping the fact she had no lights on within had hidden her in the darkness. For a moment she wondered if perhaps she wouldn't have been glad if he'd seen her. At least then he would know she was interested in what was going on. At least then he may have smiled at her, winked at her, encouragingly.

Jacey sat on the kitchen floor, her back against the wall, her head in her hands. Four years had passed, and Scott was neither married nor seeing anyone seriously. Surely it would have been one or the other if he'd been able to move on from what they'd shared at such a young age. Wouldn't he have? The little ember of hope that had been glowing off and on inside Jacey's soul began to smolder again. Jacey closed her eyes, remembering the look on Scott's face earlier in the day when it was announced Megan had purchased him in the sale. It was an expression of hidden anger, irritation, and fear. Maybe Nora was right. Maybe Scott would just fall back into Jacey's arms if she asked him to. Maybe… maybe the night he'd asked for her forgiveness wasn't him asking for her forgiveness at all. Maybe he'd been lying when he'd thanked her for forgiving him, told her he'd "dealt" with it, and it was finally over. Maybe he'd been lying as much as she had been lying when she hadn't told him the truth: that she was still in love with him, always would be.

"Okay, everybody," came Carla's voice over the loudspeaker in the courtyard, "it's midnight. Servants are officially free to sleep, or whatever, until nine a.m."

Carla's announcement caused a wave of relief to travel over Jacey. Megan would have to keep her hands off Scott for at least nine hours. The first day was over. Two to go. Again Jacey assured herself Megan couldn't win Scott over in just two days.

She heard the front door open and was glad Nora had returned. She needed some company.

"Nora," Jacey said, still sitting on the floor, "did you have fun?"

"Why are you sitting in the dark?" It was Scott's voice in response.

Leaping to her feet, Jacey's heart began to frantically pound within her chest.

"Oh!" she exclaimed. "I...I...I didn't want the light from the apartment to be distracting. You know...with the dance going on and all."

"Hm," he said, tipping his cowboy hat back on his head a bit as he looked around. "Harbine here?" he asked. Jacey shook her head, and Scott nodded. "I've come to kill him," he explained. Shaking his head, he looked at Jacey and said, "This is hard for me, Jace. I don't know if I can take two more days of this. She had me shopping at the mall all day! Can you believe that?" Jacey couldn't help but grin, remembering how Scott loathed shopping. "And it's not funny," he said, pointing an index finger at her. "I had to pretend I was her boyfriend the entire time...holding her hand, waiting on her hand and foot like some...some..."

"Indentured servant?" Jacey finished for him, seething at the thought of Scott holding Megan's hand all day.

"Exactly," Scott sighed, realizing his predicament. "I feel like a piece of meat," he told her. For all her heartache and hidden jealousy, Jacey couldn't help but smile.

"Like a kept man?" she teased.

"Yeah," he said, shaking his head as he ran a hand over his face and scratched the fiveo'clock shadow at his chin for a moment. "She's a nice enough girl," he added, causing enraged jealousy to catch in Jacey's throat. "But she's kind of...bossy and ditzy at the same time. The entire situation just makes me want to mangle Harbine or to...or to..."

Without further warning, Scott's hand went to Jacey's throat, encircling it with a firm gentleness as he pushed her back against the wall. The act startled Jacey, and she gasped, breathless, as Scott's mouth crushed her own. His kiss was wet, driven, almost brutal—as if he meant to entirely devour her! She could do nothing but accept him, match his ambitious affectionate assault. Her hands went numb, her toes tingled, and her heart soared as he kissed her.

Although it ended nearly as suddenly as it had begun, he seemed as breathless as she was when he whispered, "Would you have bid on me today?" Jacey's mind fought for stability. Still in a state of complete delirium, she couldn't seem to fully surface from what had just happened between them. "If Megan hadn't bought me outright?" he asked, still breathing heavily. "Would...would you have bid on me, Jacey?"

There it was, the fear, gripping Jacey's heart. Fear of rejection, fear of further heartache. But for a fleeting moment, faith mingled with hope, and she managed to whisper, "Yes."

His eyes narrowed. He studied her face intently for a moment and then nodded. "Okay," he breathed, still nodding, still studying her face. "Then I have to leave now."

Without one more word, without a hint of what was going through his mind or what had caused him to act so impulsively, Scott straightened his hat, said, "'Night, ma'am," and left.

Her knees already weak from Scott's advances, Jacey put her hand to her throat and sank to the floor. What had just happened? Her mind fought for answers, explanations for Scott's impulsive, incredibly passionate advance on her. *He still loves you!* she thought. She wanted to believe it! Part of her even did. She thought over the past few weeks, of their mutual confessions the first night Scott had moved in with Harbine—their confessions of never having gotten over one another, his revealed reasons for having broken up with her in the first place. He still loved her! Her heart was telling her so. The same heart that had so painfully ached over him for so long was willing to leap for him again.

Jacey tried to catch her breath, brushed tears of hopeful joy from her face. Perhaps...perhaps she would find the courage to go to him. But doubt immediately began preying upon her thoughts once more. Fear and doubt, the devil's tools, disheartened her nearly immediately as she thought of Megan and her remaining two days of owning Scott.

And Scott would fulfill his commitment. Whether he thought it was a wise thing or not, Jacey knew once Scott Pendleton had given his word about something...he'd follow through. For a moment, Jacey considered leaving for the two days, missing classes even, to run home and hide from the sight of Megan in Scott's company. Surely at home it would be more easily endured than watching firsthand. And what of the second half of the Indentured Servant Sale? Jacey had committed to being auctioned off! Would anyone bid on her? Would Scott? What if someone bought her outright the way Megan had Scott?

All too quickly, the spark of hope trying so desperately to fan in Jacey's soul began to flicker dangerously, close to being snuffed once more.

"That kiss," Jacey whispered to herself, closing her eyes as Nora's words on a previous occasion echoed in her memory. "That was not an 'it's really over' kiss. That was an 'I'm having trouble not whisking you to the bedroom' kiss," Jacey whispered to herself, remembering what Nora had said about the night Jacey and Scott had supposedly found their closure to the past. Was it true of the kiss she'd just shared with Scott? She sensed it was. She wanted to believe it was. But apprehension still dominated her emotions. She was still too weak from so many years of carrying a broken heart.

Sleep was the only way to find respite, and Jacey knew it. There were still two more days to endure Megan's flirtations with Scott. Once it was over, however, Jacey would have to choose a path: the path of strength or the path of weakness. Strength would find her courageous, pursuing Scott herself. Weakness might find her without him forever. But for the time being, all Jacey could do was fall into bed, the feel and taste of Scott's kiss still heavy in every fiber of her being.

CHAPTER SIX

Over the next two days, Jacey tried to stay out of Megan and Scott's way. The more she thought about the night of the sale—the night Scott burst into her apartment and nearly devoured her in an impassioned kiss—the more she tried to buoy her courage and hope.

Still, it proved difficult. Especially each time she'd catch a glimpse of Scott in Megan's company, her hand attached to his arm, her head flirtatiously leaning against his shoulder. Scott would reassuringly wink at Jacey every time he'd see her with Megan on his arm, and it did give Jacey a little hope.

Midnight was fast approaching. Midnight and the end of the first half of the indentured servant rouse. Five minutes to midnight found Jacey, Nora, and Harbine crouching behind the shrub near Megan's apartment, waiting for Scott to walk Megan home. It would be the end of his obligation, and Jacey wanted to see it end. She wanted to see Scott walk away from Megan. For some reason, she needed to see him walk away from her.

"Nora," Harbine whispered, "can I take this rag off my head at least?"

"Shhh!" Nora shushed him. "Yes, yes, yes. Your pirate days are over, babe."

With a heavy sigh of relief, Harbine pulled the red bandana from his head. "I don't know what you two are worried about," Harbine grumbled, stripping off the red long coat as well. "For three days our dude there has been near to tearing his hair out because of Megan. She about drove him to the nuthouse."

"Shhh! Here they come," Nora whispered. "Hold still, Harbine! You'll give us away."

Jacey smiled as she saw Nora reach down and pick up a small pebble, tossing it in hand several times before looking back to where Megan and Scott now stood at Megan's apartment door.

"You're a good sport, Scott," Megan told him, smiling. Jacey inhaled deeply and tried to remain calm as she watched Megan reach out and begin to toy with one of the buttons on Scott's shirt.

"You're a generous woman," Scott said in return. "I can't believe you gave that much to the cause."

Megan giggled and said, "It was a chunk, I admit it. But you were well worth it."

Jacey looked to Harbine, who was obviously irritated and wrinkled up his face while mouthing, *But you were well worth it.*

"Well…I hope you had fun," Scott said.

"I did," Megan said, still fiddling with the button on Scott's shirt.

"Good night then, Megan," Scott said, and Jacey smiled, relieved—but only momentarily. For in the next instant, Megan rather brazenly took hold of the front of Scott's shirt, fisting the fabric of it in her hands as she pulled him closer.

"Two grand, Scott," she said. "For two grand… don't you think I deserve a kiss?"

"Um…Megan…you're a sweet girl and—" Scott stammered.

"One kiss, Scott," Megan interrupted. "It's…it's the traditional way to end this thing. Everyone does it."

"I'm gonna nail her head to the ground!" Nora said, letting her pebble go.

"You missed!" Harbine scolded as the three spies watched the pebble disappear into the night without hitting its intended victim.

"Megan, I…I don't think…" Scott began. Jacey listened intently. It was obvious he was uncomfortable, but Megan was right. The indentured servants always gave a good-bye kiss when it was asked of them.

"I know you've probably got your eye on someone, Scott," Megan began, "and that this was maybe a little difficult for you. But all I'm asking for is one good-night kiss…one two-thousand-dollar kiss."

Jacey held her breath and sensed Nora and Harbine did too as they waited for Scott's answer.

"Megan," Scott said, shaking his head slightly.

"Shhh," Megan told him, putting a finger to his lips. "We'll keep it our little secret, Scott." And with that, Jacey watched in horror as Megan raised herself up on her tiptoes and pressed her lips to Scott's. Scott did not pull away. In fact, he put a hand to Megan's cheek and kissed her in return for a moment. Nothing intimate, nothing beyond a tender kiss shared between friends, but it was enough to cause Jacey's heart to constrict with anger, hatred, jealousy, and heartbreak.

Any courage she'd managed to build toward pursuing him, toward opening her heart to him again, was smashed as she watched Scott pull away from Megan. He'd kissed her! He'd kissed her with the same lips he'd kissed Jacey with two nights before.

"Dude, Jacey," Harbine began in a whisper, "it's just the tradition. That's all. It didn't mean anything."

"Every kiss means something," Jacey choked.

"This is just between friends, Jacey," Nora told her, "like if you were to kiss Harbine...which, I might add, you have."

"This isn't the same, Nora," Jacey said as tears began to spill from her eyes.

"Jacey, don't do anything you're going to regret," Nora warned, placing a hand on Jacey's arm.

Jacey yanked her arm away from her friend's touch and watched as Scott touched the brim of his hat and said, "Good night, Megan."

"Good night, Scott," Megan said. She went into her apartment and closed the door behind her. Scott turned and began walking toward the shrub on his way to his own apartment.

Jacey reached down and picked up a handful of pebbles. Standing up, she threw the small projectiles at

Scott, and then he shouted, "Hey!" while covering his face with his forearm.

"You jerk!" Jacey cried. "You jerk!"

"Jacey!" Scott exclaimed. "What are you doing?" he asked as Harbine and Nora stood as well. His eyes narrowed as he realized they had been watching him. "You were spying on me?"

"You're a jerk!" Jacey choked through clenched teeth. "How could you kiss her like that? Huh? How could you?"

"She asked me to," Scott said. "She—"

"Nora," Jacey said, brushing tears of anger and pain from her cheeks. "Ask him to kiss you. That's all it takes. You ask him…he kisses you! Go on, Harbine! Give it a whirl!"

"Dude, Scott…will you kiss me?" Harbine asked. But Scott just clenched his jaw and continued to glare at Jacey.

"Shut up, Harbine!" Jacey said, picking up a handful of pebbles and throwing them Harbine's way.

"Jacey…come on," Nora tried to soothe. "It's…it's the tradition. It doesn't mean anything."

"It means everything, doesn't it, Scott?" Jacey asked. Her chest burned with agony; it rose and fell dramatically with the labored breathing of anger. "Isn't that what you once told me? Huh? Isn't that what you always told me, Scott? That a kiss is the most—"

"Jacey," Scott interrupted, "how much did Harbine pay for you last year?" He was angry as well. The fire in his eyes was proof of it. "How much, Jace?"

Jacey didn't answer, her anger keeping her from understanding why the question was relevant.

"Eight hundred big ones, dude," Harbine answered.

"That has nothing to do with—" Jacey began.

"And for eight hundred bucks...did you kiss him when it was all over?" Scott asked. "Because he's a nice guy and treated you well and became your friend...did you kiss him, Jace?"

"That's...that's completely different," Jacey stammered as her mind struggled to embrace the concept of Scott's defense of himself.

"Is it? How?" he asked, striding toward her. He stood towering over her, glaring down at her, infuriated. "How? How is that any different, Jacey?" Jacey brushed more tears from her cheeks, sniffling as he continued, "She's a nice girl, and she treated me well. She didn't try anything on me, didn't expect anything all that outrageous. Two grand, Jace. You kissed Harbine for eight hundred bucks. She put down two grand...and you think I'm over the line."

Jacey knew he was right, but the vision of Scott kissing Megan, no matter how innocently it was meant to be, was making her insane. She looked to Nora and Harbine, desperate for support in her own defense.

But as Nora raised her eyebrows, Harbine simultaneously shrugged his shoulders and said, "He's right, Jacey. I mean...in truth...you sold out for less than he did, dude."

It didn't matter what anybody said. It had still been like a knife through the heart, seeing Scott kiss Megan.

"Night crawlers, my rear end," Scott said, suddenly remembering a similar scene that had transpired involving the same shrub. "You guys weren't looking for night crawlers out here the other night. You were spying on me then too!"

"Whatever," Jacey mumbled, suddenly horrified he'd put two and two together. She guessed then the temperature must be dropping, for she began to shiver almost uncontrollably. Though it seemed as the shiver began deep within her and spread out, rather than the other way around.

"Why were you spying on me, Jacey?" he asked, reaching out and taking her chin in hand. "Why are you so ticked off at me for giving that girl one friendly kiss? Hmm?" When Jacey only continued to glare up at him, he added, "Tell me why."

Jacey's mind silently cried, *Because you're supposed to be mine! I should be the only one you ever kiss!* Instead she moved to slap him, but he easily caught her wrist before her hand met his face. Catching her free hand as she began to struggle, he forcefully pinned her wrists at her back.

"Let me go!" she growled through clenched teeth, struggling to break free of him.

"Just tell me why you're so ticked off and upset," he growled in response, pushing her back against the brick wall behind her. He managed to hold both of her wrists at her back with one of his hands, using his body to further restrain her by pressing her against the wall, while taking her chin with his free hand.

"Say something to me," he growled. "Just…just say something to me, Jacey."

But she couldn't. Her anger was dissipating, for he was right. He'd kissed Megan in a dramatically less familiar manner than Jacey had kissed Harbine the year before. It was an obligatory kiss, and Jacey knew it. Further, she had no claim on him. The past was the past, and she'd done nothing to try to win him in the present. What right did she have to be angry?

"Just…just let me go, Scott," she whispered then. "Please. I'm sorry. I…I don't know why I went off at you like that. You're right. You're right."

Jacey felt Scott release her wrists at her back, but he continued to hold her chin in hand, his eyes narrowing as he looked at her. "That's it?" he asked. "That's all you have to say to me?"

"I…I guess," she stammered. She watched as Scott's jaw visibly clenched. She heard his teeth grinding together with irritation.

"Fine," he said. "I've been very patient, Jacey. But…I'm tired of it. I'm tired of trying to do what's right instead of what I want to do." Jacey remembered his having said the same thing before. She remembered how delicious his kiss had been that night several weeks ago when he'd said it and then kissed her. "I'm tired of it," he repeated. "So…let the games begin!" He released her then, straightening his shoulders. "Good luck tomorrow," he told her. "You'll need it."

He turned and began walking away, leaving Jacey confused, fatigued, and awash in self-loathing. *I'm a coward*, she thought to herself. She closed her eyes, and a vision of herself hiding behind a shrub, instead of walking straight up to Megan and laying claim to Scott before Megan had ever had the chance to kiss him, flashed through her mind. All of it, all of it was her fault. Fear had won her over in the end, and she would pay the price of cowardice forever.

"Dude," Harbine called after Scott, "I was just kidding about asking you to kiss me."

Jacey watched as Scott dropped a two-fingered peace sign at his side to let his friend know all was well.

"Jacey," Nora began, "what is wrong with you?"

Jacey brushed the tears from her cheeks and said, "I know. I know."

"You just blew him off, Jacey!" Nora reminded her. "You just…you just let him go. You didn't even try to—"

"I…I can't take it again," Jacey whispered. "I can't. I think I'd die if I tried…if he left after—"

"Dude," Harbine began, putting a heavy arm across her shoulders. "He's ticked," he said, stating the obvious. "He's tried not to…not to upset you, you know."

"He upsets me by just walking across the lawn," Jacey told her friend.

"No, but he's really ticked this time, Jacey," Harbine repeated. "He's tired of messing around. He's not gonna pussyfoot around you anymore."

"So I gather," Jacey said.

"I mean, he's going to charge ahead...bet the farm...go for broke," Harbine added.

"She gets the point, Carl!" Nora exclaimed.

"No," Harbine said. "I don't think she does."

"What do you mean by that?" Nora asked.

Jacey looked to Harbine, puzzled as well. Did he mean Scott was done with her...or did he mean something else?

"Time will tell, won't it?" he answered. "All I'm saying is...you need to get past this fear that's holding you back, Jacey. Get past it, or it's gonna control you forever. It'll ruin your life if you let it."

Jacey ran her fingers through her hair, knowing Harbine was right. He was right. She didn't have to be told how dangerous fear was; she already knew. Still, the vision in her mind of Megan and Scott kissing...it was horrific.

"Why did he have to kiss her though?" Jacey asked. "Why did he have to kiss her?"

Harbine put a heavy hand on each of Jacey's shoulders. He grinned a grin of understanding and compassion and said, "Same reason you kissed me last year, dude...obligation." He reached out and took one of Nora's hands in his, raising it to his lips and kissing the back of it adoringly. "Obligation and the path to heaven's grander purpose."

Jacey put a hand to her temple as Harbine gathered Nora in his arms and began to place loving kisses on her neck and cheeks. "I'm completely done," she said. "Completely. I'm going to bed."

"I'll be there in a minute," Nora said.

"Take your time," Jacey told her. At least someone was happy—happy, adored, and loved.

Jacey's head was pounding like a drum was penned up inside it, but her hearing was fine. For a moment she wished it weren't when she passed Megan's apartment and heard her telling someone, "I'm certain Scott's going to bid on me at the sale tomorrow! Maybe he'll purchase me outright even!" An eruption of recognizable giggles let Jacey know Megan had been talking to Steph.

"Great," Jacey muttered. As if it couldn't get any worse, she'd forgotten about the fact the second half of the Indentured Servant Sale began the next morning. Not being stupid enough to hope Scott would bid on her after what had just happened, she felt nauseated at the thought he might actually bid on and win Megan. He was "tired of it," he'd said. "Let the games begin," he'd said. And what better venue to take in getting on with life than with a person who was already in your net?

Once again, Jacey fell into bed puffy-eyed and emotionally and physically drained. She wondered if she would ever feel happy again. She wondered if her stomach would ever stop burning and churning, if her heart would ever stop feeling as if it were on the verge of giving out. She wondered what Scott would do with Megan if he bought her. Would he kiss her again? More thoroughly this time? Jacey winced at the thought.

"He's still yours, you know, Jacey," Nora softly said

as she entered the bedroom. "You know it's true. Deep down inside, you know it. Don't give up on yourself just because of this. There's still time to reach for the brass ring."

Jacey sniffled and said, "Maybe." She closed her eyes and thought about Nora's encouragement—about Harbine's. She thought about the tender autumn quote Scott had found in the dental office magazine— the way he'd carried it in his wallet—saved if for her. She thought of the photo Harbine had taken that first evening Scott had appeared, the way he'd been looking at her. She thought of his face, the dread and disappointment so apparent on it when he'd realized he'd been purchased by Megan. She thought of his asking her if she would've bid on him, of his kiss—his passionate, wonton, promising, loving kiss…the kiss that spoke and tasted as much of love and devotion as ever it had when they were younger.

Jacey dreamt then of a carousel. She rode a golden pony, and each time she would circle, she would see Scott, holding one hand out to her, a brass ring clutched tightly in his fingers. All night she rode, round and round and round. With each round of the carousel, Jacey attempted to reach for Scott, tried to capture the ring in his hand. Round and round and round she rode, all through the night. Once or twice her fingertips touched the brass ring Scott was holding. Once or twice in her dream, he said, "Jump, Jacey. I'll catch you. I promise."

It was Nora's soft snore that woke Jacey in the

morning. She still felt tired, as if she'd truly been riding the carousel all night, arms sore from reaching out for Scott. Yet somehow she wasn't as fearful as she had been the night before. Miraculously the tiny ember of hope buried deep in her had not grown completely cold, and it burned a little warmer than it had the day before.

Jacey could hear activity in the courtyard, everyone getting ready for the second half of the Indentured Servant Sale. Fear began to creep into her mind, but she fought it, drawing from the memory of her dream. *Jump, Jacey*, Scott had said in her dreams. *I'll catch you. I promise.*

CHAPTER SEVEN

Jacey watched Scott's expressions as Carla announced Megan was up for auction. Scott had not made eye contact with Jacey all morning. No sideways glances, no friendly smiles, no reassuring winks. It was obvious he was still angry too—for the set of his jaw was firm, and Jacey could tell his teeth were clenched.

"I give you Megan Tannis, ladies and gentlemen!" Carla announced from the podium. The men began to whistle and clap, and Jacey turned away as she saw Scott applauding as strongly as any other man in the audience.

"He's going to bid on Megan, Nora," Jacey whispered. Her hand went to her stomach, trying to calm the nervous rumbling inside.

"No," Nora said. "He won't. He'll still bid on you. You watch."

"I can't," Jacey said. "I'm going to be sick."

"Get a hold of yourself, Jacey," Nora told her. "Just wait and see."

"Do I have an opening bid?" Carla was saying.

"A hundred," a man's voice called out.

"A hundred dollars! Thank you, Mr. Emery!" Carla said. "A hundred once…"

"One fifty!" another man shouted.

"One fifty from Mr. Christiansen!" Carla announced.

"You see, Jacey?" Nora said, smiling. "It's going to be between Ben and Braden, just like Harbine said."

Jacey inhaled a deep breath and dared to look out from behind the curtain. Scott still stood next to Harbine, his arms folded across his chest as he watched the goings-on. A subtle frown puckered his brow for a moment, and he leaned over, whispering something to Harbine.

"Do I have two hundred?" Carla asked. "One fifty going once…"

"Two hundred!" Ben Emery shouted.

"Two fifty!" Braden Christiansen countered.

"Three!" Ben shouted.

"Whoa! Three hundred dollars! Three hundred dollars has been offered to help the orphanage at Christmas in Megan Tannis's name! Gentlemen, three hundred once, three hundred twice…"

"Three fifty!" Braden countered.

"Three fifty!" Carla repeated. Jacey still watched Scott's face. Perhaps he still meant to bid on her. Perhaps he was just waiting until the price went up so he could flatter her with a higher bid. "Three fifty once, three fifty twice…"

Jacey drew in her breath as Scott again leaned over

to Harbine and said something as he pointed toward the podium.

She couldn't breathe, holding her breath until Ben shouted, "Four hundred!"

"Five hundred!" Braden countered without waiting for Carla to announce the previous bid.

"Five hundred, ladies and gentlemen!" Carla exclaimed. "The current bid stands at five hundred... the highest bid of the morning so far! Gentlemen...five hundred going once, five hundred going twice..."

"Breathe, Jacey!" Nora exclaimed in a whisper. "You're going to pass out!"

"Sold!" Carla exclaimed, dropping her gavel to the podium loudly once. "Sold to Braden Christiansen for five hundred dollars!"

Jacey watched with guilty relief as Megan forced a smile when Braden bounded like a happy puppy up onto the stage.

"Thank you, Braden," Carla began, "for your generous contribution in purchasing Megan's indentured servitude." Carla turned to Megan. "Megan Tannis," she announced, "having sold yourself into servitude for a period not to exceed, but no less than, three days and three nights...you must agree to do your master's bidding. Each and every task asked of you."

"I agree," Megan said, finally displaying a sincere smile as Braden took hold of her hand.

"Braden...enjoy your girl! Megan Tannis and Braden Christiansen, ladies and gentlemen!" The crowd cheered, whistled, and applauded, and Jacey finally let out the breath she'd been holding. She knew she would've simply passed out backstage if Scott had bid on Megan. Only she and Nora remained, and he hadn't bid on Megan. Harbine would buy Nora, but that didn't mean Scott would bid on Jacey. Still, at least he couldn't bid on anyone else.

The crowd grew restless waiting for Megan to return from the dressing booth. Jacey waited, anxiously nervous, wondering whom Carla would call up next. After a few minutes, Megan did appear dressed in a French maid's costume very similar to the one Jacey had worn the year before.

The crowd cheered and applauded, and Jacey grinned slightly, glad Megan looked pleased with Braden. She took his arm, and they smiled at one another. She was a nice girl. Jacey felt bad for harboring such ill feelings toward her.

"Settle down, gentlemen. Settle down," Carla began. "Our sale continues with another indentured servant. Next up on this afternoon's agenda…Jacey Whittaker!"

"Oh, no!" Jacey muttered as Nora pushed her from behind. Jacey stumbled out onto the stage, and the men in the crowd roared. She dared a glance at Scott. He was still frowning, arms still folded tightly across his chest.

"I give you Jacey Whittaker, gentlemen!" Carla said once the roar had died down. "Three days and three nights with Jacey Whittaker as your indentured servant, boys!" Carla called out. "Seventy-two long

hours of telling her what to do and what to wear…"
The whistles and shouts from the crowd caused Carla
to add, "All within reason, boys! Remember…all within
reason and the rules."

"Do I have an opening bid?"

"A hundred bucks!" someone shouted. "I'll start it
at a hundred bucks!"

Jacey didn't dare to look at Scott, but she knew it
wasn't Scott who had started the bidding. She tried to
smile, tried to still the trembling in her hands and legs,
tried to look pleasant.

"A hundred bucks?" Carla repeated. "My little sister
makes more than that babysitting!"

Jacey resisted the urge to run, to put her hands to her
cheeks to cool her blush. What had she been thinking
by getting roped into such a ridiculous situation again?

"Two hundred!" Ryan McKay called out. "Two
hundred!"

Jacey sighed, slightly relieved. Ryan was a good guy,
a good friend. He wouldn't work her too hard or try
anything inappropriate with her. Still, she could not
bring herself to look at Scott. Was he glaring at her,
daggers of hatred spitting from his eyes?

"Two hundred! That's more like it!" Carla said.
"Two hundred once…"

"Five hundred," Jacey's heart began to race at the
sound of his voice. Her heart nearly stopped when
she found the courage to look at him. She felt like an
overfilled balloon was swelling in her bosom, light and
ready to burst.

"Five hundred? Are you serious?" Carla asked. When Scott nodded at her, Carla smiled and said, "All right then! I have five hundred for Jacey Whittaker! Five hundred once…"

"Six hundred," Leonard Kendall countered. Jacey's heart sank. Leonard Kendall had the worst fish breath Jacey had ever smelled. He was always flirting with Jacey, and she was always kind to him. Still, his dyed black hair and pallid complexion always made Jacey uncomfortable.

"Six hundred dollars, ladies and gentlemen!" Carla announced. "I have six hundred dollars on the table for Jacey Whittaker. Six hundred once…"

"Eight hundred," Scott calmly countered. Jacey felt a smile begin on her face. He wasn't simply upping the ante each time by fifty or a hundred dollars; he was upping it by a couple hundred.

"Eight hundred," Carla said. "I have eight—"

"Nine," Leonard said. "Nine hundred."

"Nine, ladies and gentleman," Carla said. "I have nine—"

"Fifteen hundred," Scott said, and Jacey's eyes widened.

"You're jumping the bid by six hundred, Scott?" Carla said, putting her hand over the microphone for a moment as she leaned over and addressed him.

"Yep," Scott said, nodding. He still had not looked at Jacey, however, and she was disconcerted about the fact. She suddenly realized perhaps he knew how high

Leonard would go and was simply going to drop out after Leonard's next bid.

"All right," Carla said, turning back to the microphone. "I have fifteen hundred dollars on the table for Jacey Whittaker, gentlemen. Fifteen hundred once, fifteen hundred twice—"

"Two thousand!" Leonard shouted, glaring at Scott.

"Oh, no," Jacey felt herself breathe. The rules for a bid of two thousand dollars or more were very specific. If someone bid two thousand dollars or more and won a candidate, the candidate was bound to share a passionate kiss with the buyer. Jacey's stomach heaved at the thought of kissing Leonard Kendall. Her entire body joined her hands and legs in trembling, wondering if Scott were mad enough at her he'd simply pushed the bid up to teach her a lesson.

"Two thousand dollars!" Carla exclaimed. "Ladies and gentlemen, Leonard Kendall has just bid two thousand dollars for Jacey Whittaker! You know what that means. This year…one way or the other…we're going to have a master's kiss!" The crowd erupted into shouts, whistles, applause, and laughter. Jacey wondered if her legs would continue to support her.

"Two thousand dollars, Scott!" Carla said. "What do you say to that?"

There was a pause as the crowd grew silent. Jacey looked to Scott, her eyes beginning to fill with excess moisture. Was he simply playing with her mind, leading her helplessly into a terrible situation with Leonard, trying to teach her a lesson of some kind? Or was he sincere in his bidding? Would he outbid Leonard and rescue her from a terrible fate?

"Two thousand once, two thousand..." Carla began.

Finally Scott looked to Jacey, simultaneously holding up one hand.

"Are you...are you outbidding, Scott?"

Scott nodded, held up his thumb and two fingers, and said, "Three."

The crowd went wild, and Jacey's hand flew to her mouth to cover her gasp. Fighting to keep tears from escaping her eyes, she drew in several deep breaths and tried to calm herself.

"Scott? Are you serious?" Carla asked into the microphone.

"Of course," came Scott's calm response.

"Th-th-three thousand dollars, ladies and gentlemen," Carla stammered. "I have a bid of three thousand dollars from Scott Pendleton for Jacey Whittaker. Three thousand once, ladies and gentlemen. Three thousand twice...Leonard?" Jacey looked to Leonard to see him shake his head, smile, and step aside. "Sold! Jacey Whittaker has been sold for three ththousand dollars!" The crowd roared as Scott sauntered up onto the stage.

"Sir, you own the note on Jacey Whittaker. She's your indentured servant for three days!" Carla announced. "Furthermore, for your generous contribution to the event...your three days begin with the master's kiss!"

"Kiss! Kiss! Kiss!" the crowd began chanting.

Jacey couldn't look at Scott at first. She felt humbled, shy, unworthy. But as the crowd continued to chant, he walked to her, putting his strong hands at either side of her waist and pulling her flush against his body. His touch was like the embodiment of heaven, and as the crowd again began to cheer once more, Jacey was forced to look up at Scott.

"Scott, I—" she began.

"You shoosh," he demanded. Then looking to Carla, he asked, "She has to do whatever I say, right?" The crowd began whistling and demanding a kiss again.

"Within reason…yes," Carla confirmed.

"Good," Scott said, still not smiling. "Then you start it," he told Jacey.

"What?" Jacey gasped.

"Don't you think she should start it?" Scott called over his shoulder to the crowd. The crowd erupted into every kind of agreement, and Scott looked back to Jacey. "You start it," he repeated. "And make it look good too."

"Jacey!" Harbine called from the audience. "You are in such deep—"

"Harbine!" Nora scolded from behind the curtain.

"Better get started, Jacey," Carla urged. "I still have Nora to go."

Jacey looked to Scott. Finally a mischievous grin was spreading across his face. Still she paused, frightened and uncertain as to what his intentions were.

"Are…are you going to push me away or something?" she asked him.

"Jacey," he breathed, frowning at her as if he couldn't believe she'd asked him the question. "Just take a deep breath. You start it. I'll take care of the rest."

Again the crowd began to chant. Jacey bit her lip for a moment as she stared into Scott's eyes. Surely he did not mean to humiliate her in front of everyone. Tentatively she took his face in her hands, slowly pulling his head toward hers. Her mouth began to water, ravenously desirous as she realized she would know his kiss again.

Softly she pressed her lips to his, kissing him lingeringly but very carefully.

"Oh, come on, Jacey!" Carla said from the pulpit. "You can do better than that!" The crowd agreed and began shouting for a better kiss. Jacey was embarrassed, frightened, and began to pull away from Scott. True to his word, however, Scott took care of everything.

"Oh, no, you don't. You're not gonna chicken out on me now," he said, and before Jacey could even gasp, she was in Scott's arms. Without any pause or restraint, his mouth captured hers, owning her completely. Moist, hot, familiar, his kiss showed no distain for her, no cruelty. After several long moments, several long, impassioned passes at her mouth, Scott released her, turned to the crowd, and said, "It's a start."

The crowd roared, and Scott bowed, saying, "Thank you. Thank you very much," in his best impersonation of Elvis. "Harbine!" he called, and Jacey watched as Harbine tossed a duffle bag to Scott. Smiling rather devilishly, Scott held the bag out to Jacey. "Better get dressed now, angel," he said. "All these formalities are cutting into my three days!"

Jacey felt as if she were walking about in a dream as she entered the makeshift dressing booth. Had Scott really doled out three thousand dollars for three days with her? Had he really kissed her the way he had in front of the entire apartment complex? Was he…was he going to give her another chance?

Hearing the impatient crowd outside, she hurriedly opened the duffle bag to reveal its contents were white, silky, and gossamer, and feathered too.

"No way," she breathed, delighted as she pulled the silky white chemise and white gossamer nighty-robe out of the banged-up athletic bag. Quickly she removed the everyday clothes she was wearing, pulling the soft chemise over her head. It was modest enough, made of white satin and not at all sheer or transparent. It had sweet little shoulder-capping sleeves and hung down to just above her knee. Jacey giggled, knowing full well what the costume was representative of. Carefully, she slipped her arms into the sleeves of the short, gossamer nighty-robe, fluffing the feathers at the sleeves and hem. The feathered hem of the diaphanous robe met the hem of the chemise perfectly, even though Jacey suspected they had not been purchased as a set.

Reaching further into the bag, she withdrew a length of white lace and ribbon with a Velcro fastener at each end. She placed the little lace and ribbon choker at her throat and quickly fastened it at the back of her neck. Lastly, she removed from the bag a pair of white, fluffy-feathered, high-heeled slippers.

Slipping her feet into them, she studied herself in the standing mirror of the dressing booth. She shook her head, smiled, and whispered, "It's a sexy angel costume!" The reality of it all was finally beginning to sink into her fevered mind. Scott had paid three thousand dollars for her! He could've more easily and much more cheaply prepurchased her as Megan had him. But he'd been making a statement by not doing so. The sexy angel costume in the bag further encouraged Jacey. It had always been her favorite nickname. Of all the ones he'd used when they had been together in the past, "sexy angel" was her favorite.

She giggled out loud, remembering the look of pure mortification on her mother's face the moment little Jacey had taken the stage in her special angel dress costume so many years before. She remembered the way Scott, only eleven years old, had put his arm around her shoulder after the Christmas pageant, after her embarrassed mother had scolded her mercilessly… how he'd put his arm around her and told her she'd looked beautiful.

"You were the most beautiful angel up there, Jace," he said. "All those other girls can only wish they were a sexy angel like you!"

Smoothing the chemise and drawing in a deep breath of courage, Jacey stepped out of the dressing booth and into public view. Instantly the crowd cheered! Catcalls and whistles erupted like Mount Saint

Helens. Jacey smiled when a broad, perfectly delighted smile spread across Scott's face as he looked her up and down.

"Nice!" he said.

"And there you have it!" Carla announced. "Ladies and gentlemen…I give you Scott Pendleton and his sexy angel, Jacey Whittaker!" Jacey smiled, realizing Scott must've told Carla about her costume while she was changing. She looked up at Scott, gazing into his handsome, beloved face.

"All this could've gone easier on you and my wallet," he said, taking her hand and pulling her toward him. "But you always prefer to go at things the hard way." He bent quickly, planting a broad shoulder in Jacey's midsection and lifting her onto it effortlessly. Once he'd situated her on his shoulder, smoothing the back of the chemise down to ensure her modesty, he clamped one strong arm at her knees to steady her, turned, waved to the cheering, whistling crowd of young men, and carried her down off the stage.

"Nice job, Pendleton," Ryan McKay said as Scott carefully let Jacey down from his shoulder. "Three grand! I can't believe it!"

"Yep," Scott said. "No eating for a year!" Jacey's smile faded as she realized what an expense three thousand dollars was to a college student. Almost an entire semester of tuition! The entire value of a lot of the cars parked in the complex parking lot.

"I'm just kidding," Scott told her, noticing the pucker in her brow.

"But—" she began.

"Shhh," he said, putting an index finger to his lips and nodding toward the stage. "The drama ain't over yet." Jacey glanced to the stage, puzzled, delighted, as she felt Scott take her hand and lace her fingers with his own the way he'd so often done years before. "Watch this," he told her.

"Ladies and gentlemen," Carla began, "now that Scott Pendleton is headed for debtors' prison, I give you…Nora Whitman!" The crowd shouted and applauded as Nora stepped out onto the stage, Harbine spinning his ping-pong bidding paddle in delighted anticipation.

"Let's start the bidding at—" Carla began.

"A thousand dollars!" Harbine shouted, raising his paddle. "A thousand dollars and I win!" he shouted, tossing his paddle over one shoulder, picking up the athletic bag at his feet, and bounding up onto the stage.

"A thousand dollars?" Carla stammered. "Harbine!" she scolded as Harbine took Nora in his arms and began smothering her with kisses. "Harbine! You have to wait until I say 'sold'!"

Harbine paused in his affectionate assault on Nora long enough to snatch the gavel out of Carla's hand and speak into the microphone.

"Going once, going twice…sold!" Harbine said, smacking the podium with the gavel. Everyone cheered, delighted by the antics of their favorite eccentric tenant. Harbine raised his fists in the air and began trotting around the stage as if he'd just won the world heavyweight boxing championship. After a few rounds about the stage, followed by a couple of bows, Harbine handed a giggling Nora the athletic bag he'd brought with him.

"Get to it, babe!" Harbine said. "I'm an impatient man!" The crowd cheered, and Nora headed for the dressing booth.

"He's unbelievable," Jacey laughed. "All right, Harbine!" she called.

"You haven't seen anything yet," Scott told her, letting go of her hand so he could join the applause. The moment he let go of her, the moment Scott was no longer touching her, Jacey began to feel nervous, felt her short-lived confidence begin to wane. Consciously she reminded herself he'd paid three thousand dollars to purchase her at the sale, passionately kissed her in front of everyone, and put an incredible amount of thought and effort into her costume. Surely it wasn't all for nothing.

Inhaling a deep breath of courage, Jacey returned her attention to the stage, where Harbine stood, grinning like he'd just won the lottery. Everyone began talking among themselves. Scott, however, seemed nervous—distracted.

"You know something I don't," Jacey said as she studied him. He was agitated and kept mouthing things to Harbine.

"That I do, sexy angel girl," he chuckled. "That I do!"

A few moments later, Jacey looked to the stage as

a ripple of whistles and applause traveled through the crowd.

Jacey gasped and exclaimed, "Oh my heck!" as Nora stepped from behind the stage curtain dressed in a beautiful white wedding gown and veil. In her hands she nervously clutched a bridal bouquet of fresh flowers. Her cheeks were rosy, and Jacey could see tears welling in her eyes. "Oh my heck!" Jacey repeated.

"Dude!" Harbine called to Scott as Nora approached him.

"Dude," Scott said, pulling something out of his jeans pocket and tossing it over the crowd into Harbine's hand. Jacey gasped again, her mouth gaping open in astonishment as she watched Harbine take Nora's hand and drop to one knee before her. The crowd went wild—cheering, whistling, and applauding, only quieting down when Carla brushed a tear from her cheek, unfastened the microphone from the podium, and held it down in front of Harbine's mouth.

"Nora Whitman," Harbine began. Jacey felt tears trickling over her own cheeks as she watched tears spill from Nora's eyes. "Nora Whitman," Harbine began again, "I love you more than life itself. Will you marry me?" There was complete silence as not a soul spoke, waiting for Nora to speak instead.

Nodding and brushing tears from her cheeks with the blossoms of the bouquet she held in her hand, Nora said, "Yes! Yes! You know I will!"

Harbine exhaled a heavy sigh of relief and

thankfully placed his forehead against Nora's hand a moment before standing and taking her in his arms.

"Ladies and gentlemen," Carla announced, brushing tears from her cheeks, "I give you the future Mr. and Mrs. Carl Harbine!" The crowd cheered like nothing Jacey had ever heard before. Jacey's own hands were sore from clapping, her eyes blurry with her own tears of joy for Nora and Harbine.

"That concludes the sales for today, everybody!" Carla shouted into the microphone as people rushed the stage to congratulate Harbine and Nora. "See you all at the dance tonight…in the courtyard, starting at nine!" Carla then abandoned her post to throw her arms around Nora's neck in congratulations.

Scott took hold of Jacey's hand again. "Come on," he said, pulling her toward the stage. "Let's get up there." Jacey followed him up onto the stage, hoping she wouldn't twist her ankle, for the feathered, high-heeled slippers were awkward under the circumstances.

"Dude! She said yes!" Harbine greeted Scott, first striking hands with him and then pulling him into a bear-hug embrace.

"Congratulations, man!" Scott said.

"Jacey!" Nora exclaimed, causing Jacey to turn around. "Can you believe it?"

"Oh, Nora!" Jacey giggled, tightly embracing her friend. "I'm so happy for you! It's so perfect. All of it! What a doll Harbine is!"

"I opened that bag and saw this dress and…and… didn't know what to think!" Nora said.

"Looks like I'll have to find a new roommate," Jacey said, brushing a tear from Nora's cheek.

Nora laughed through her tears and said, "Haven't you found one already?"

"What?" Jacey said, even though she knew Nora was implying she might be lucky enough to find herself in Nora's shoes, Scott on his knees before her instead of Harbine.

"And what's all this?" Nora said, taking Jacey's hands and pulling back to study Jacey's costume. "It looks like Scott's ahead of Harbine in his intentions today!" Nora turned Jacey around and giggled. "Did you see the 'Sexy Angel' written across your bum in gold cursive?"

"What?" Jacey exclaimed. Quickly she tugged at the back hem of the chemise. Sure enough! There on the back of the chemise were printed the words "Sexy Angel" in gold cursive. Jacey laughed and turned back to her friend. "Oh, Nora! I'm so happy for you," she said. "You two are perfect together!"

"Thank you, Jacey," Nora said, hugging her friend again.

"Away, you plebeians," Harbine said, brushing people aside dramatically as he returned to Nora. "I must whisk my betrothed away to seclusion now!" Jacey laughed as Nora's already broad smile broadened.

"I'll see you later," she said a moment before Harbine picked her up in his arms and lumbered away.

"'Bye!" Jacey called after them. It was wonderful! All of it! She felt selfish, realizing she was even happier for herself in what the events of the day had brought than she was for Nora.

"I love that guy," Scott said, moving to stand beside her.

"Yes," she agreed. "He's incredible."

"Well," Scott sighed, "I'll be in bed…waiting for you."

"What?" Jacey exclaimed, her attention instantly pulled away from Harbine and Nora. Her mouth gaped open in astonishment.

"I'll be in bed…waiting for my breakfast," he explained. "It's only nine-thirty, and I haven't had my breakfast yet. You're to do my bidding for the next three days. Let's start with breakfast in bed."

"Oh," Jacey said, sighing, relieved. "I thought you meant…I thought you were teasing about…"

"I know," he said, smiling at her. "But I told you last night…I'm tired of messing around, Jace." He leaned toward her, kissed her quickly on the mouth, and added, "The games have begun, my pet." He turned and began walking away. "I'll be in bed…waiting for you," he called over his shoulder.

Jacey blushed scarlet as a low, "Whooooaaaa," emanated from the crowd around her.

"And don't forget the bacon," Scott added.

"He…he just wants breakfast," Jacey stammered as twenty sets of raised eyebrows met her. "That's it."

Turning to follow Scott, she glanced back to where Harbine was carrying Nora toward the apartment. Her heart swelled with happiness, delight in the obvious and profound joy of her friends. They so very greatly deserved the magnificent love they'd found.

Jacey turned and walked quickly along the path Scott had taken. She would make him breakfast—the best breakfast of his life! Complete with an entire pound of bacon all to himself.

The sun seemed brighter as she mounted the steps in her fluffy-feathered, high-heeled slippers. She fancied the air was fresh, for she felt her breathing was lighter than normal. Everything seemed brighter and lovelier, from the early autumn breeze to the leaves changing from green to crimson on the trees.

"He was so nervous," Scott said as Jacey entered his apartment. He chuckled. "I thought he was going to explode this morning, he was so nervous."

Jacey smiled as Scott handed her a pound of bacon from the refrigerator. "I can well imagine," she told him.

"I made pancake batter already," he said. "And if you take Harbine's straw out of the syrup...I think there's enough for both of us."

"I thought you wanted breakfast in bed," Jacey said, smiling lovingly at him.

"Naw," he said. "I just wanted to embarrass you. And it worked too."

"It did," Jacey laughed.

"But I do expect a morning kiss with my orange juice," he said, winking at her.

"Seems to me you already had your morning kiss," she told him, "out there in front of everyone."

"Maybe," he said, his eyes narrowing as he looked at her for a moment. "Now get to fixing my breakfast, sexy angel servant."

Jacey smiled—blissful in his company—hopeful in what might transpire between them over the next three days. A flame of faith and hope flickered within her. She could feel fear moving to the corner of her mind. Still, it lingered, and as she looked at Scott, she was reminded of what a magnificent man he'd become, and she fought to keep the flame of hope burning.

"Harbine," Scott chuckled as Jacey set a skillet on the stove. "What a riot!"

CHAPTER EIGHT

With the exception of having to attend a few classes, which couldn't be missed, Jacey spent the entire day with Scott. He was talkative, polite, funny, and relaxed. It seemed as if the awkwardness that had hung so heavily between them since he'd arrived had all at once begun to dissolve. They talked and laughed over breakfast and then lunch, reminiscing about events that had taken place in high school and around the neighborhood at home while they were growing up. He told her about his first three years in college, his injury, and his decision not to play football anymore. She told him about her senior year in high school, starting college, and meeting Nora. They enjoyed pleasant conversation together for hours and hours, just the way they'd used to.

Little by little, Jacey began to feel more comfortable being with Scott, more relaxed in his company. However, once in a while she'd still catch herself studying him, suddenly intensely aware of how large he was in stature, how much more handsome he was— even more so than he had been as a teenager. Moments like these found Jacey's insides churning, her thoughts lingering on her unworthiness in comparison.

Yet each time he'd smile at her, laugh at something they were discussing, or share a confidence, Jacey's heart began to warm. The flicker of hope within her began to grow, and she found herself wondering if maybe winning him again weren't all that unfathomable.

Scott had a late class that first night, preventing him from spending dinner with Jacey. Jacey took the opportunity to freshen up a bit before the dance, scheduled at nine in the courtyard, and to talk to her darling Nora about her engagement.

Nora seemed to be walking on air—dazzled by the fact she was to be Harbine's wife. She explained to Jacey that although she'd kept it a secret, cached it deep within her soul, she'd been dreaming of marrying Harbine since the day she met him. They had already decided the wedding would take place in December, knowing long engagements were never emotionally healthy, and Jacey burst into tears when Nora asked her to be maid of honor. For all the excitement and joy Nora shared with Jacey, it was understandable it would be Harbine Nora wanted to be with most that day. Therefore, Jacey's time with her friend was brief but wonderful.

As the DJ finished setting up his equipment in the courtyard, Jacey prepared for the dance. Scott said he would be at her apartment at nine to pick her up. And so she ran a cool iron over the white chemise she was bound to wear, washed her face, and reapplied fresh makeup.

Standing in front of the mirror, Jacey studied herself for a moment. She wondered if she'd changed and matured as much in appearance as Scott had. Sighing, she inwardly admitted she hadn't. She didn't look much different than she had at age seventeen or eighteen. It was a fact of life girls reached full maturity at a younger age than boys. Still, it didn't seem fair Scott should have changed so much physically. Jacey smiled, however, thinking of the events of the day and how familiar it had all seemed, of how familiar Scott had seemed. If she could only get past being intimidated by his obvious maturity and astounding good looks! Would things progress between them? Perhaps it would take time—a long time even—but Jacey began to thrill at the hope that had begun to burn brighter in her mind and heart.

Gathering her hair in one hand at the back of her head, Jacey twisted and pinned it into a French twist. She liked to think wearing her hair up made her appear more sultry and sophisticated. She shook her head, realizing sultry may have been more easily accomplished than sophisticated, considering her silly costume.

She heard a knock on the apartment door and giggled with delight, realizing it was nine. It would be Scott, she was certain. She stepped into her fluffy-feathered, high-heeled slippers and tried to appear unruffled as she opened the door.

A delighted smile spread across her face, and she even sighed as Scott said, "Hey, baby. Are you ready?"

"Yeah," she said, though her knees felt weak just looking at him.

"Let's go then," he said, reaching down and lacing the fingers of one hand with hers. He smiled as he led her to the courtyard where the DJ had started the music. Several couples were already dancing, and several girls were gathered around Harbine and Nora. "Ohhs" and "aahs" of admiration were escaping the mouths of the girls admiring Nora's engagement ring. Jacey smiled and thought of the lovely ring on her own right ring finger, the one Scott had given to her the night he'd moved in with Harbine. She consciously realized then she'd never taken it off for a moment since. She envied Nora, wearing the ring of the man she loved on her left ring finger—the visible promise Harbine meant to own her.

"Everybody is totally stoked they're getting married," Scott said. "Especially you, huh?"

"Yeah," Jacey admitted. "I remember the first time Harbine saw Nora," she told him. "I was dressed up in that ridiculous French maid costume, cleaning his kitchen. It was the last day of the indentured servant thing last year. Nora came up to tell me my mom called and wanted me to call her right away. Nora left, and I turned around to see Harbine sitting on the couch with his mouth hanging open." Jacey paused, a fit of giggles rippling through her as she thought of the scene. "I remember he had been eating crackers and spray cheese, and there were crumbs all down the front of his shirt. 'Dude, Jacey,' he said. 'Dude…your roommate is the woman of my dreams!' I didn't know him as well then as I do now, but thinking back on it," she said, looking up to Scott, "I think he was serious that day. I always thought he was just being dramatic. But…but now…I think he meant it."

"I know he did," Scott said, smiling and glancing back to Harbine. "Aren't you glad you endured wearing that outfit and cleaning his rank apartment so they could meet?"

"I am," Jacey said, smiling.

"And aren't you glad I wiped out my entire savings and bought you today?" he asked. His eyes narrowed as he brushed a strand of hair from her cheek.

"I…I…I am," she managed to admit. There! She'd done it! Taken the first step toward the possibility of having her heart broken again. In that brief moment, Jacey had consciously decided the old adage was still true: it was better to love and to lose it again than never to have gone for it in the first place.

As if having read her thoughts, Scott took her hands in his and began backing onto the dance floor. There was a pause before the next song began, and he said, "I feel like a swimming instructor leading a hydrophobic into deep water."

"What?" Jacey said, though she already knew what he meant. Still, she didn't want to confirm his suspicions she didn't trust him not to break her heart again.

"You know what I mean," he chuckled. "You're afraid to trust me. I get it. I didn't at first, I admit it. I was too distracted by my own...issues. But I get it now. You have to learn to trust me all over again. And I have to understand it and be patient."

Even if she could've fathomed a response, suddenly overwhelmed with nerves, delight, fear, hope, and something like brief disorientation, Jacey did not have a chance, for Harbine and Nora stepped up next to them.

Harbine put his hands at Nora's waist and said, "I dedicated a song to you, my fluffy kitten."

Jacey looked from Scott to her friend and grinned as Nora's broad smile spread across her lovely face.

"What's that, handsome?" Nora asked.

"You'll see," Harbine told her. "It works for Scott and Jacey too," he added.

"Really?" Scott said, smiling. "Slow or fast?"

"Slow, dude," Harbine said, scowling. "Give me a break." Harbine pulled Nora against him and nuzzled her ear. Jacey couldn't help but giggle as the goofiest of love-struck grins overtook his features. "An oldie...but a goodie," he said.

"I had to dig pretty deep for this one," the DJ announced. "But here it is...going out to Nora from Carl." Nora tossed her head back and laughed as the first few, very recognizable notes of "Endless Love" grew into the night.

Scott smiled and high-fived Harbine as tears welled in Nora's eyes as she said, "I love you, Carl."

"I love you, baby," Harbine said, kissing Nora sweetly on the cheek.

Jacey shuddered, suddenly very emotional as Scott put one hand at her waist. Tentatively, she placed a hand at his shoulder as he took her other hand in his and began to dance with her. The euphoric and long-absent sensation of dancing with Scott was intoxicating! Pure enchantment drizzled over Jacey like a warm, sweet pastry frosting. She wanted to reach out, take his face between her hands, and kiss him long and hard on the mouth!

However, the first drop of rain to land on Jacey's forehead and trickle down the bridge of her nose distracted her. She looked up at the same time Scott did, blinking when another raindrop fell into her eye.

A general moan of disappointment groaned from the crowd when the DJ said, "Gotta cut it short, kids! Looks like rain!"

"Come on!" Nora exclaimed as the clouds overhead released a burst of showers. "Our apartment is closest!"

Taking Jacey's hand, Scott pulled her along behind him as he rushed toward the apartment. By the time the two couples were safely inside, the rain was merciless in its downpour.

"Bummer!" Harbine said. "Lionel and Diana didn't get to finish their song for us, Nora! I'm sorry."

Nora just giggled and hugged Harbine, saying, "It's all right, babe. You can sing it to me yourself around the bonfire at the lake tomorrow night."

"You guys spending the day at the lake with us

tomorrow, dude?" Harbine asked Scott. Scott rather collapsed onto the sofa, and Jacey took a seat in the old recliner across from him.

"Of course," Scott confirmed.

Jacey smiled as a mass of butterflies seemed to take flight in her stomach. All day with Scott, uninterrupted by classes or any other responsibility—it would be fabulous! She looked at him, and he winked at her.

"And I suppose I can let you change out of that sexy angel costume long enough to change into a bathing suit and go swimming," he told her.

Jacey was suddenly uncomfortable; every woman was at the prospect of appearing in a bathing suit before a man she adored. Short or tall, fat or slim, Jacey had never known a girl who was comfortable in the "swimsuit" situation. For a moment she considered fabricating a fear of the water but remembered Scott would know better. They'd spent days and days and days at the lake or the pool in the summer as kids. He knew she enjoyed the water. He'd taught her to swim when she was five, for Pete's sake.

"So, Jacey," Scott began. He looked tired. He continued to lean back on the couch and appeared as if he might fall fast asleep if he closed his eyes for more than a few consecutive moments. Already self-conscious, Jacey's nervousness escalated as he grinned and asked, "Do you prefer hairy chests or bare chests?"

"Wh-what?" Jacey stammered, looking to Nora, who raised her eyebrows and smiled with amusement.

"On men, I mean," Scott explained. "Do you

prefer hairy chests or bare chests? 'Cause, depending on your answer…there's still time before we go to the lake tomorrow."

"I-I…" Jacey stammered. She could feel the hot crimson on her cheeks, the butterflies rising in her stomach. In the past, the seemingly far-away past, she would've simply answered Scott. No pause, no consideration—just an answer. She wondered at how the question would've been so much easier to answer when she was sixteen—when she had been younger, more innocent, lighthearted, trusting, and entirely comfortable with him. Now, however, there was more to consider. Four years ago, Scott had been only nineteen, and although he'd been mature for his age, well-built, and gorgeous, he had been younger, and he'd seemed much younger—younger than the taller, more strikingly handsome, intimidating man who now slouched back on the sofa before her. His shoulders had not been as broad, his jaw not nearly as squared, and suddenly Jacey could not remember clearly the condition or lack thereof concerning his chest hair. At first she wondered if he'd had chest hair at all. In her completely rattled and entirely nervous state, she tried to evoke a vision of the way he'd appeared the last time they'd gone swimming together. Swallowing the lump of nerves in her throat and reaching back in her memory, she was able to calm herself enough to remember that Scott had indeed had some chest hair when they were younger.

This then posed a new problem. What if his chest

hair had increased in profusion and thus he'd rid himself of it? Chest hair or no chest hair? Would the wrong answer hurt his feelings? As she sat stammering, struggling for just the right words, Scott chuckled and slipped his hand under the hem of his shirt, pushing it upward to reveal his well-sculpted stomach and chest.

"I mean...if this is too much for you, I still have time to wax," he said with a wink. "I'm sure it would hurt... but I can take it." Jacey's attention was involuntarily drawn to Scott's exposed torso, and she felt the crimson already burning her cheeks begin to increase.

"No!" Jacey gasped, entirely unsettled by his exposure. "I mean...I mean to say...chest hair is the general preference. Isn't it, Nora? In...in moderation, I mean?"

Harbine chuckled. "Dude...you're freaking her out."

Nora smiled, no less than absolutely delighted by Jacey's discomfort. Jacey glared at her friend as Nora giggled and answered, "Yes. Yes...I believe chest hair, in moderation, is the general preference."

Harbine pulled at the neck of his own T-shirt, looking down inside to his own chest. "So what do you consider 'moderation,' Nora?"

Nora giggled again, reached up, and twisted a finger in a lock of Harbine's hair, saying, "You're fine, babe. Just perfect."

"This isn't too much then?" Scott asked, suddenly pulling his T-shirt off over his head and running his hand over his chest as he looked at it. Jacey gasped and nearly leapt from her seat in the old lounge chair. "'Cause…if this isn't moderate enough for you, Jace," Scott continued, "I have a beard trimmer, and I could pop the number six attachment on and go over it a couple of times to sort of thin it out and—"

"No, no," Jacey interrupted, holding a palm toward him as if she expected him to whip out a razor and begin grooming his impressive chest at that very moment. "That's—that's fine. It's fine," she nervously stammered. Jacey had never in her life seen such a well-sculpted torso! In the movies maybe, but not in real life. It rattled her completely, especially with Harbine and Nora grinning, wholly amused at her expense.

"Dude!" Harbine chuckled. "Just get her right now! Just grab her and lay one on her! Right on the mouth! She's too freaked out to run."

Jacey narrowed her eyes, glaring at Harbine, as she growled, "I am not freaked out." Still, she gasped and hopped to her feet when Scott did stand up from his seat at the sofa and take hold of her hand.

"You better tell me, Jace," Scott said, grinning impishly at her as he held her wrist, rubbing her palm over his chest. "I want to make sure you're comfortable."

"Do it, dude!" Harbine said. "Plant one on her now before she runs off! Otherwise it's like eating Crunch 'n Munch and not finding any peanuts. Totally frustrating, dude."

"Harbine!" Jacey rather barked, glaring at her friend. Her cheeks hurt, the blush on them was so intense.

"But he's right," Scott said. "What's the point of Crunch 'n Munch without peanuts?" With that, Scott gathered Jacey into his arms as his head descended toward hers. "You know how it is, Jacey," he said, his voice low, the intonation that of syrup. "You open a box of Crunch 'n Munch, reach in…" He pulled her tightly against his body and let his lips hover just above hers. "And what's the first thing you do?" Jacey's mouth flooded with moisture, thirsting for his kiss.

"Start digging for peanuts!" Harbine exclaimed.

"Exactly," Scott whispered. Jacey couldn't help but smile. Although she was still nervous, trembled in Scott's arms, the analogy Harbine had introduced and Scott seemed to fully understand was too delightful.

"Three thousand bucks, Jace," Scott said. "Ain't it worth one peanut?"

"You mean…like the two-thousand-dollar peanut you gave Megan yesterday?" Jacey said. Somehow the anger that had riddled her the day before over the kiss Scott had given to Megan had dissipated. Smiling, she was able to tease him about it now without the anger burning her throat. It still bothered her, but she understood it…accepted it.

Still, Scott breathed a heavy sigh and said, "That wasn't a peanut. That was a hull."

"Yeah! A nasty old hull," Harbine added. "Like the one that gets stuck between your teeth…way down in your gum, like…and you start bleeding while you're trying to get it out using the corner of your dad's business card or something."

Scott chuckled, and Jacey couldn't help but giggle at Harbine's eccentric outburst.

"Harbine!" Nora scolded in a whisper. "You're distracting them!"

"Oh," Harbine said, adding in a whisper, "sorry, dude."

Scott smiled at Jacey as he shook his head. Then brushing her lips lightly with his own, he whispered, "Come on, Jace…just one peanut. Three thousand dollars certainly should've earned me one peanut. Right?"

In the next moment, he was kissing her, carefully, slowly, and without heavy demands. Shy, uncomfortable in front of Harbine and Nora, Jacey pulled away from him.

"Come on, Jacey!" Harbine exclaimed. "That's popcorn…not peanuts!"

"Harbine!" Nora scolded again.

"Don't listen to him," Scott said, taking Jacey's chin and directing her face back toward his as his mouth descended against hers once more. This time the ambitious kiss he started could not be denied, and Jacey melted against him, allowing herself to return the affectionate exchange.

"Niiiiccceee!" Harbine said as Scott finally broke the seal of their lips.

"I'll let you climb back in the box, Jace," he whispered, affectionately tweaking her nose. "For now." He kissed her cheek and turned to go, leaving Jacey weak-kneed and blissful.

"Dude," Harbine said, kissing Nora on the mouth and standing to leave as well. "See you later, baby," he said to Nora. Then putting an arm up and around Scott's shoulders, he said, "Dude, tomorrow…you should go for almonds!"

Once the boys had exited the apartment, closing the door behind them, Jacey collapsed into the old recliner.

"It's building, Jacey!" Nora exclaimed. "You guys are going to—"

"Don't say it out loud, Nora," Jacey interrupted. "You might jinx it." Jacey's heart was aflutter—her body tingly—her brain numb. Hope was flaming within her bosom. She was beginning to think maybe dreams could come true twice in a lifetime.

"Okay then," Nora said, reaching out and taking Jacey's hands in her own. "Then I'll be selfish!" Leaping to her feet, she pulled Jacey out of the chair and squealed, "I'm getting married! Ahhhhhhhhh!"

Jacey laughed and squealed as well, hugging Nora as they hopped around like two little girls who had just won tickets to a Justin Timberlake concert.

After ridding themselves of their indentured servant costumes, Jacey and Nora laid in bed talking far into the night. Colors, flower arrangements, and menus were discussed. Jacey tried to listen intently but found her mind constantly wandered to what her own wedding might be like one day…to visions of Scott as the groom…visions of her lifelong dream finally coming true.

CHAPTER NINE

The day spent at the lake had been fabulous! Scott had been playful, flirtatious, and completely attentive. Megan had even remarked to Jacey it seemed as if Jacey had purchased Scott at the sale rather than the other way around. Swimming, boating, sunbathing—all of it had been a much-needed break from the pressures of regular, everyday life.

Furthermore, Jacey had awakened that morning with a newfound courage. The events of the day before had given her the strength to believe that Scott still cared for her and that he might be obtainable after all. It was a giant leap of faith, she knew, but Jacey had awakened that morning faithful and ready to jump.

She smiled as she looked down at the couples sitting around the bonfire near the lake's edge. The breeze was sweet and cool, breathing of summer's end and autumn's debut. She closed her eyes and smiled, inhaling the scent of the night, the serenity of the moment. With a contented sigh, she tossed her bag into the back of Scott's pickup, smiling as she thought of tossing her high school backpack into the bed of the same old red pickup so many times in that beautiful past they'd shared. Holding the high-heeled slippers in one hand, she smoothed the satin chemise, fluffed the feathers at the sleeves and hem of the nighty-robe, secured the Velcro fastener of the white lace choker at her throat, and turned to head down toward the water's edge.

"Where you going?" Scott asked, smiling as he jogged over, throwing his own bag into the back of the pickup. Jacey smiled, pleased at the sight of him. It was funny, the way the girls spent an hour primping, redoing hair and makeup after a day at the lake, while the men simply remained in their shorts or bathing suits, tousled hair, and neglected sunburns.

"Down to the fire," she said as he went to the driver's side of the pickup, opened the door, and began rummaging around inside.

"Why?" he asked. As music began to pour from the speakers inside the pickup, Scott nodded to Jacey and said, "Wanna open that other door?" Jacey smiled as she heard the old '50s version of "Smoke Gets in Your Eyes" drift from the pickup's sound system. She opened the passenger side door, and Scott turned up the stereo volume. Everyone down at the fire began to clap and whistle, pleased with the music.

"What?" Jacey teased. "The lap of the water, the music of the crickets, the crackle of the fire…it's not enough sound for you?"

"Sure it is," he said. "Sometimes." He walked around the pickup and unlatched the tailgate. "But not tonight." He took hold of her at the waist and effortlessly lifted her to sit on the tailgate. Hopping up beside her, he sighed and said, "It was a fun day, huh?"

"It *was* a fun day," Jacey said, smiling at him. She sat her heeled slippers next to her and sighed to herself as she studied the scene before them. The lake was still, like black glass reflecting only the stars and moonlight. Couples around the fire were engaged in various activities—some roasted marshmallows, some were drawing in the sand, and some, like Nora and Harbine, were cuddled up in each other's arms.

"So tomorrow is the last day of ownership," Scott said with a dramatic sigh, followed by a dazzling smile. "After tomorrow night…you're a free woman."

Jacey's heart landed with a thud in the pit of her stomach, but she forced a smile and said, "I guess so. And I guess that means I can wear something…normal from now on."

"Why would you want to do that?" he chuckled. "You look so good in this!" He reached out and plucked a loose feather from one sleeve of the gossamer robe. "Hmm. Come to think of it," he began, spinning the quill of the feather between his thumb and index finger and winking at her, "you'd probably look even better out of—"

His words were stopped as Jacey clamped her hand over his mouth and exclaimed, "Don't be naughty!" A blissful tingle began at her palm where it touched his mouth. It quickly traveled up her arm, filling her entire body with delighted warmth. She felt him lick her

185

palm, and he chuckled as she promptly dropped her hand from his face. Butterflies erupted in her stomach, and every inch of her flesh broke into goose bumps as he smiled at her.

"You've been a good sport, Jace," he said, his eyes narrowing, his smile fading a bit to an approving grin.

"Well," Jacey sighed, smoothing the satin of her chemise again, "it was for a good cause. Charity and all." She giggled as he laughed.

"Actually, all the girls have been good sports about it," he said, looking down the hill to the bonfire. Jacey grinned as she followed his gaze. Although her costume was definitely the most negligee-ish, it was not nearly the skimpiest or the most unusual. She raised her eyebrows as she studied Steph, thankful Scott had not asked her dress up like one of the characters from the Broadway version of *Cats*.

"Well, I'm just glad you didn't make me dress up like a feline," Jacey said, smiling at him.

He shook his head and said, "No…just my sexy angel." He winked at her, and she felt the familiar stab of anticipated heartache pinch in her chest. She looked away for a moment, back to the fire and the couples there. He wouldn't break her heart again. She was sure of it. At least, that's what she had been telling herself all day.

The Righteous Brothers began to croon "Unchained Melody" into the night air, and Jacey asked, "Why did you buy me, Scott? Why…why did you go to all this trouble?" She mustered enough courage to look at him.

She needed to hear him say it, needed to hear him tell her out loud he still cared for her.

His smile had completely faded, his eyes narrowed again, and he said, "It was for a good cause—charity and all." Jacey looked away, trying to fight off the fear threatening to come out of its corner.

In days gone by, Jacey would've simply pressed him for a more definitive answer, confidently begged him to further explain. But now…now she was afraid, afraid of what the true answer might be, and so an uncomfortable silence hung in the air between them as the music played.

Jacey closed her eyes, letting her mind, her memory, drift back to other nights…nights spent sitting on the tailgate of Scott's pickup, watching the sun set or the lake sleep—less nerve-wracking nights when talking led to cuddling, cuddling progressing to blissful moments of being held in Scott's arms, sharing bliss-filled kisses.

She managed, somehow, to withhold her tears, and her eyes opened as Scott slid off the tailgate, taking hold of her hand.

"Come on," he said as she slipped from the tailgate. The sand and grass felt cool beneath her feet. The breeze whispered over her body, simultaneously relaxing and revitalizing. Jacey's hand began to tremble, her senses intensely conscious because of his touch.

"Where?" she asked him.

"Just up here," he said, leading her up the slight incline to the crest of the hill, "to the top of the hill."

Once they reached the top of the hill, he put his

arm around her shoulders, turning her to look down the opposite side of the hill to the grassy meadows below, the starry sky above.

The Righteous Brothers still sang with the evening breezes. Scott removed his arm from Jacey's shoulders, took one of her hands in one of his, and said, "Will you dance with me?"

"H-here?" Jacey stammered.

"Yeah," he said, grinning at her as he turned her to face him. "We really didn't get to do it last night. The rain saw to that."

Many were the times in those memories Jacey so often dreamt of when Scott would drive her out to Murdock's Hill, turn the pickup stereo on, and dance with her out under the stars. But those days were over. Jacey loved them, but they were over. The memories of dancing under the stars were just memories. Weren't they?

She looked at Scott, dressed in nothing but his board shorts, her in her sexy-angel costume. She smiled, remembering the way he'd teased her about her hairy or non-hairy chests preference the night before. Dancing on top of this hill, under these stars, wouldn't be like it used to be. But maybe…maybe that's not what he intended. Maybe he really did just want to dance; they'd started to the night before at the apartment complex dance. Maybe he just wanted to sway to the Righteous Brothers as they unchained a melody.

"Okay," she said. A wonderful shiver traveled up her spine as he put one of his strong hands firmly at her waist, taking her other and pressing it to his chest. Oh my heck, he was dangerous! The handsome, beguiling grin spreading across his face as he began to sway back and forth with her would be any woman's undoing!

Almost instantly, Jacey regretted agreeing to dance with him. His manner and his movements were so familiar, so desperately desirable, and it was different than it had been the night before. The solitary seclusion set an entirely different mood. Again, the likewise familiar burn of withheld tears stung Jacey's eyes, and she looked past him, over his shoulder into the night.

"It's…it's almost over, you know," she told him as she heard the Righteous Brothers winding down.

"I know," he said. "But there's another one after this."

Jacey wasn't sure whether she should rejoice or despair. She wanted nothing more than to stay in his arms, feel the warmth of his body next to hers, assured he existed and wasn't just a dream. Still, she wondered if her emotions could endure the pressure, wondered if her heart could endure it. He'd told her the night before he meant to earn her trust again. Wasn't it an implication he meant to have a relationship with her? Surely it was. But Jacey wondered if she would be able to keep her tears of hope and trepidation under restraint so he would not know how desperately she still loved him…would always be in love with him. Surely, she did not want him to know how perfectly he still owned her heart, not when he was taking everything so slow.

As the Righteous Brothers faded away, Scott

continued to sway as if he knew the music would start again in a few moments. However, the moment the first strains of the next song began, Jacey's breath caught in her throat, and she stopped matching his sway, stepping back out of his grasp.

"I—I can't…" she said. Fear and desire mingled in her veins. She couldn't dance with him! Not to "At Last"! It was one of her favorite songs…one of her favorite "think of Scott and cry" songs. The memories crashing through her mind, sparked by the first few notes of the song, were overwhelming. It had been "At Last"—the last song they'd ever danced to. It had been Etta James's emotional rendering that had danced Scott out of Jacey's life the night they'd broken up. Etta James had been singing "At Last" from Scott's pickup the night he'd told her he had to let her go. It had been the song playing as he'd driven away from her, leaving her alone and so entirely broken.

"Yes. You can," Scott said, taking one of her hands in his. He stepped closer to her but did not try to force her into a dance position. He simply began to sway ever so slightly, patiently waiting for her to join him.

Tears stung Jacey's eyes, and she swallowed the need to release them. Slowly she began to match his sway, his pause, and his step as Etta crooned "At Last."

Tentatively, Scott placed a hand at her waist, slowly pulling her closer as he continued to sway with her. Still holding her hand, he bent, brushing her cheek with his own. Slowly moving his face across hers, he lingeringly brushed her other cheek with the other side of his whiskery face.

Etta's soulful voice still sang as Scott's hand released Jacey's, traveling caressively up her arm, over her shoulder, coming to rest at her neck. Tenderly he held her neck with one hand as his other left her waist, sliding up over her back, under her arm, and over her shoulder to rest on the other side of her neck. The Velcro fastener at the back of her neck, the fastener of the white lace choker, pinched her slightly as Scott's hands held her, his thumbs caressing her throat.

Jacey was instantly breathless as she felt Scott use his thumbs to ever so slowly push the soft lace of the choker upward, revealing the hollow of her throat. She gasped as he bent, placing a moist kiss there. Instantly her hands went to his chest, weakly pushing against him in an effort to stop the spell he was weaving about her.

"Scott," she breathed.

"Sshhh," he whispered in return, placing another kiss on her throat. Jacey closed her eyes as Scott's thumbs pushed at her chin, directing her head backward. His fingers fumbled with the choker for a moment. Finally, he simply reached around, loosening the Velcro and pulling the thing off completely. With the lace of it held between his fingers, his hands again encircled her neck as he began placing lingering, moist kisses on her throat.

Jacey thought she might faint dead away as Etta James finally breathed the last line of the song. She was breathless, near to melting, her knees shaking as Scott pulled her against him then. He held her tightly in his arms, his cheek pressed to hers, his breath tickling her ear as the music stopped. Again, his body did not cease in swaying with hers as the music ended, but Jacey was too wrapped in the euphoria of the dream come true to reason why.

It wasn't until Scott's voice so near her ear began singing "Love Me" as Elvis's drifted from the pickup that she melted against Scott, finally succumbing to his enticements. It was too much. She wanted the past to be tangible once more! She wanted her dreams to come true again. She wanted Scott to seem real again, be hers again, even if it proved to be only for an instant in time.

Letting her hands caress the breadth of his shoulders, she held his neck between her hands—never wanting to release him. Softly he kissed her neck—let his lips caress her cheek as they traveled toward her mouth.

Jacey's entire body rippled with goose bumps as he sang against her mouth.

He took her mouth with his then, his kiss soft, tentative at first. Quickly, however, Jacey found her body willingly crushed against the power of his as their kiss grew into a slow yet ravenous mingling of intimate emotion.

She belonged to Scott! She had to own him! As Jacey returned his kiss, as their mouths mingled in the unrestrained affectionate exchange, she knew she could never give him up. Never!

She felt him lessen the force of his embrace, felt

his hands at her waist, tightly holding her, his thumbs digging almost uncomfortably into her ribs as they continued to kiss.

Slowly breaking the seal of their kiss, he said, "Initially, I had decided to…to ease you into this, Jace," as he gazed into her eyes. "I-I figured we had to build on something completely new…without the past as part of it. I knew I should give you time…time to trust me, time to figure out if you could still…if you could still love me. But the past will always be part of it, Jace. Because that's where it began…and it really never did end…did it?"

"N-n-no," Jacey sniffled as he softly brushed her tears from one cheek with the back of his hand.

He smiled and seemed to sigh, relieved. "Last year I was in the hospital…after the surgery on my leg," he told her. "I had a lot of time to think, and I realized… I'd been trying not to. I'd been trying not to think for three years…not to think of my future, not to think of you. And what I realized in those moments was…that in all my trying not to think of you…it's all I did." He brushed more tears from Jacey's face, letting his thumb travel caressively over her lips as he continued, "That day…lying there in that stupid hospital bed, I thought, 'Why does everyone have to tag first love, that pure young love, as only puppy love?' Admittedly, a lot of the time that's probably what it is, but not always… and not where we were concerned. It was like someone slapped me upside the head and shouted, 'Wake up, idiot!' And I realized I'd been listening to the wrong voices…the voices of the world instead of my soul, the voice of a whacked-out mother who'd lost her way a long time ago. I realized all I wanted was to hear your voice…to hear you giggle the way you do when you think something is funny, to hear you singing the way you do when your heart is happy. All I wanted to hear was your voice telling me you loved me. So I decided to listen to my own voice for a change…that one in my head and my heart telling me the right thing to do. The one I'd been trying to rationalize away for so long."

Jacey couldn't speak. Her heart was so full of euphoric joy and love it was swelling into her throat.

"Did you ever stop loving me, Jacey?" Scott whispered, pulling her against him, swaying with the music, kissing her neck softly. "Did you?"

Jacey slid her arms around his neck and with a comfortable courage breathed, "No! Never! Not for one moment!" Scott kissed her hard on the mouth before taking her face between his hands and smiling down at her as she continued, "I…I tried. I really did! For four years I tried…but…but I couldn't! I couldn't get you out of my mind or my heart. I couldn't get you out of my soul! You own me," she confessed. "You… you always have."

Scott's mouth crushed hers in a brutal kiss. He kissed her as if a great thirst had overtaken him, one that only her mouth could quench.

Then he took her face between his hands once more and asked, "How old are you now, Jace?" She was confused. After all their confessing, for him to ask her age…it was out of context in the least.

"Um…um, twenty-one," she stammered.

He chuckled, obviously already aware of her age, yet for some reason wanting her to verbalize it. "Well, as you know, I'm pretty good with numbers…and goals," he said, smiling at her. "And I'm really good with setting goals *with* numbers." She watched as he fumbled in the pocket of his board shorts for a moment. Finally drawing something out of the pocket, he took hold of her left hand. "What was my jersey number when I played for State, Jace?" he asked, smiling at her.

Jacey shook her head, too confused and delighted by his confession of never having ceased in loving her to think rationally along any other lines. "Twenty-one," she answered. "Why?"

"And how old are you right now?" he asked, raising her hand to his lips and kissing the back of it.

"Twenty…twenty-one," she stammered breathlessly as realization overtook her. Surely he did not mean to…

In the next moment, Jacey watched, astonished as Scott then slipped a ring—a goldbanded diamond solitaire—onto her left ring finger. Tears flooded her cheeks, and her knees buckled as she was overcome with the realization of her lifelong dream coming true. Scott gathered her into his arms, holding her tightly against him as she broke into joyous sobbing.

"Will you marry me, Jacey?" he whispered against her ear. "I've been waiting my whole life to ask you. I've been waiting my whole life to hear you say—"

"Yes!" she interrupted through her breathless sobbing. "Yes!"

"I love you, Jacey," Scott said, his voice breaking with emotion.

"I love you," Jacey told him, hugging him tighter, though she thought it was impossible.

"Wanna marry me in six weeks? We could haul our old pumpkin stand out of your dad's garage and make a few bucks! Or do you want to wait until Christmas and…" he said.

Jacey pulled out of his arms long enough to look at him. She placed her palm against his whiskery cheek and said, "You know I'll always choose pumpkins over anything else, pumpkin."

Scott smiled, and Jacey frowned, puzzled as "Love Me" began anew.

"Did the CD skip?" she asked.

Scott shook his head and chuckled. "I recorded it twice in a row. I thought it might take more than once through for you to say yes."

Jacey giggled as he put a hand at her waist. She put a hand to his shoulder as he took her other hand and held it against his chest. Pressing his forehead to hers, he began to dance with her as he sang along with the song.

"I do love you, Scott Pendleton," she told him, leaning back to look up into his eyes. "I always have."

The soft, southern syrup of Elvis Presley's voice mingled with the cool autumn breeze. Scott and Jacey's kisses mingled as well—evidence of the endurance of a first and only love…an everlasting love.

Breaking the seal of their lips, Scott chuckled. Jacey could feel his smile against her neck.

"What?" she giggled as he bound her in his arms.

"That stupid song of yours keeps running through my head," he told her, still chuckling.

"Which one?" she asked, sighing as he kissed her neck.

Scott chuckled again. "That stupid Donny Osmond one—'Puppy Love.'"

"Why?" she asked, breathless in his arms.

"'Cause this never was just a puppy love!" he said.

Jacey giggled as he lifted her off her feet, spinning her around as the stars winked at them from the midnight sky above.

EPILOGUE

"Bye-bye, Charles!" Jacey Pendleton called, tossing a friendly wave at the postman as he drove away. Charles was a nice guy, always made sure Scott and Jacey's mail was delivered promptly. Smiling, she began to thumb through the envelopes in her hand.

"Mommy!" Tommy said, tugging on the hem of Jacey's shirt. "Did I gets anyfing? Did I?"

Jacey smiled, stroked the top of her tiny son's head, and said, "No, bud. I'm afraid not."

"Awwww," Tommy whined, disappointed. Yet in the very next moment he'd forgotten the letdown of not having received any mail at such a worthy age as four. The toddler hunkered down, instantly mesmerized by the trail of ants on the sidewalk beneath his feet.

Jacey giggled as the familiar handwriting on the front of one of the envelopes caught her eye.

"Tommy," she began, "run tell Daddy that Uncle Harbine and Auntie Nora have sent a picture of their new baby! Hurry!"

"I'll do it! I'll do it! I will!" Tommy said, leaping to

his feet and racing for the house. "I bet their baby is ugly compared to our baby Baylee!"

Jacey's smile broadened as she watched the little dark-haired bundle of energy run headlong for the backyard.

"Daddy! Daddy!" Tommy called as he ran. "Uncle Harbine's had a new baby! I think it's an ugly one!"

Jacey anxiously tore open the envelope and withdrew the small birth announcement within. Tears filled her eyes as she gazed at the photo of the newborn baby. With Nora's eyes and Carl's round face, the little guy was Harbine through and through.

"Oh, Nora!" she whispered, brushing a tear from her cheek. "He's beautiful!" Her emotions were mixed—great joy because of the baby's birth mingled with intense disappointment at not living near enough to hold him. Jacey missed Nora, but she was grateful the two families managed to see each other at least twice a year since they'd all gotten hitched.

Lovingly, Jacey traced the photo with her thumb, as always amazed at the miracle of birth. Turning her attention to the text of the announcement, she gasped, cried, and then laughed. In the next moment, a nearly uncontrollable laughter overtook her. She read the announcement again, just to make certain she had read it correctly the first time. Again, she laughed. She missed Nora and Harbine and their adorable children, now three in number.

When Scott arrived, baby Baylee in one arm, Tommy in the other, Jacey was still wiping tears of joy, melancholy, and mirth from her cheeks. More tears spilled from her eyes at the sight of her handsome husband toting their two beloved children.

"What's the matter, babe?" Scott asked. "Tommy said Harbine and Nora had their ugly baby."

"He's a beautiful baby!" Jacey told him, finally getting control of her tears and laughter. "But now I know why they wouldn't tell us his name on the phone the other night when they called."

"Why?" Scott asked, setting a squirmy Tommy down as Jacey handed him the photo. Scott turned his baseball cap backwards on his head and smiled as he looked at the picture of the newborn baby dressed in a tiny red-and-black State football jersey, the number twenty-one emblazoned on the front.

"Harbine always said he'd name his first son after you, babe!" Jacey said, handing the announcement to Scott.

"*The Harbine Family welcomes its newest addition,*" Scott read aloud, "*Pendleton Scott Harbine.*" Scott laughed. "No way!"

"And look here," Jacey began, taking the photograph and turning it over. "Look what Carl wrote here." Jacey pointed to Harbine's nearly illegible handwriting.

"*Pendleton Scott Harbine,*" Scott read. "*Ten pounds, three ounces…21 inches long. It's meant to be, dude! Still your biggest fan…Love, Carl.*" Jacey watched Scott's face, saw the excess moisture gathering in his eyes. "That dude is still crazy," he said, his voice breaking with emotion.

"You mean a lot to him, Scott," Jacey said, taking Baylee from him so he could study the announcement and photo more thoroughly.

"Da!" Baylee chirped, still looking at her father.

"I love you too, muffin," Scott said, kissing the top of Baylee's head as he continued to gaze at the photo of the newborn baby dressed in football garb.

"Tommy," Jacey said, setting Baylee down in the grass of the front yard, "talk to Baylee for a moment… and don't let her eat any grass this time please, sweetie."

"Okay, Mommy!" Tommy agreed, plopping down in front of his sister. "Now, baby Baylee," Tommy began, "if you're going to eat green stuff…make sure it's Jell-Os you eat…not grass."

Scott shook his head as he looked at the Harbine baby's photo once more.

"It…it seems like yesterday, Jace," he said. "It seems like yesterday we were all just a bunch of crazy college kids."

"We haven't changed very much," Jacey told him, sliding her arms around his waist and nestling into his strong embrace. She breathed deeply of the scent of him, the scent of newly raked leaves, freshly mowed grass, cedar chips, and the same cologne he'd worn since they were teenagers. Oh, how she adored him! How fervently she thanked heaven for him every night, thanked heaven for her children and the life they all lived together.

"Daddy!" Tommy whispered excitedly. "Daddy! Someone's comin' up to the pumpkin stand!"

Scott chuckled and tousled his son's hair. "Well," he said, "go sell them a pumpkin, Tom!"

"Can I, Mommy? Can I go sell them the pumpkin this time?" Tommy asked, hopping up and down like a grasshopper in a hot skillet.

"Of course," Jacey said, smiling. "But remember to be polite."

"I will! I will! Oh, I will!" Tommy said as he headed off to the pumpkin stand at a dead run.

Jacey giggled, glancing down to ensure Baylee was sitting still, safe and occupied.

"Last time I let him sell the pumpkin, the people buying it gave him a twenty and told him to keep the change," Scott chuckled.

"I love you, Scott Pendleton," Jacey said, looking up into her husband's happy, handsome face. Each day that passed, she found herself loving him more. Their life together was wonderful, full of joy, laughter, and love.

"I love you too, Jacey Pendleton," Scott whispered, pulling her into his arms once more and kissing her. His kiss was moist, demanding, and all too passionate for such a public place as their front yard.

Yet Jacey didn't care! She kissed him too, unreserved, impassioned, until Tommy shouted, "Hey! I'm trying to sell a pumpkin here!"

Scott chuckled and called, "You sell your pumpkin, boy! I'm kissing your mommy!"

Jacey smiled at Scott as he put his hand to her waist and took her hand in his other, pressing it to his chest.

Gradually he began to sway back and forth and bent, impersonating Elvis as he sang into her ear. Jacey giggled and laid her head against Scott's chest as he continued to sing.

Dreams really did come true! Jacey knew it because she was living them. She was dancing in her lover's arms, and when night fell, she would sleep in them. Her children played happily in the front yard of their home, and Nora, Carl, and their precious little ones would be visiting for Thanksgiving. Her dreams of Scott, the dreams of it all, hadn't been nearly as wonderful as the reality had turned out to be.

"Daddy!" Tommy said, tugging on the hem of Scott's T-shirt. "That man gave me ten dollars for a pumpkin, and he said he'd give me ten more if you'll kiss mommy again the way you just did!"

Scott and Jacey looked over to see one of the guys from Scott's city-league basketball team smiling as he watched them.

"What's up, Craig?" Scott called, nodding his head at his friend. "Here, baby," he said, kissing her long and hard once more. "I gotta show this to Craig," he added, waving the photo and birth announcement in the air. He started to walk away, but looking at her, he kissed her hard once more and said, "Just love me."

"Oh, I will," Jacey said as she watched him pick up Tommy and saunter over to the pumpkin stand to talk to Craig. "I always have, haven't I?"

AUTHOR'S NOTE

I think everybody has one: that "first love" we never completely get over, in one way or the other. Some of us do find a more wonderful, truer, and deeper love—yet never quite forget the heartache or sweetness of that very first love. Some of us never get over it at all, haunted by the memory of it with painful regret and feelings of loss that never go away, especially when life is throwing lemons. Still, some of us find our first love is our truest, deepest, forever love—blessed with never having had to get over it. Wherever you fit, whatever category you relate to, I think this story presses on something deep within us all.

Personally, I fit into the first category—grateful in the knowledge my first love was *not* my true love and yet never quite forgetting the rotten heartache and misery of that first love. Oh, sure, I learned a lot from it—things that taught me and helped me in all aspects of my life, especially in finding the wonderful, loving, near-perfect husband I'm so greatly blessed with. Yet first love—it's something we all experience.

I suppose these are the reasons why *Love Me* was so popular when it was first released as an e-book. I sometimes think those who find themselves thankful they didn't end up with their first love are glad someone's first love did have a happy ending. Those who never got over their first love, yet were forced to move on, find themselves escaping into a world where first love prevails. Furthermore, those who found their first love was their best and truest love probably enjoy *Love Me* because they feel a sort of kinship to it. It's all theory, of course, but I like to think it's fairly accurate.

In revealing a secret truth, I did have a friend in mind when I wrote *Love Me*. This friend falls into the second category of first love—the "never got over it at all, haunted by the memory of it with painful regret and feelings of loss, especially when life is throwing lemons" category. Let's call my friend Vanessa. Vanessa found true love at a very young age—younger than sixteen, if I recall. Let's call Vanessa's true love Johnny. Johnny was wonderful—tall, dark, handsome, romantic, polite, loving, and respectful. And Vanessa adored him. Vanessa and Johnny didn't break up because of choice; rather, other people and circumstances forced them apart. Vanessa grew up, moved on, and never, never got over Johnny—never! I think it was this haunting knowledge of my friend's eternal heartache that inspired *Love Me*. Scott and Jacey—in love since they were children and, after losing one another because of someone else's interference the way Vanessa lost Johnny, find each other again and live happily ever after. Oh, I know it doesn't change anything for Vanessa, but somehow it helped *me* feel better. Don't misunderstand me. I still get sick to my stomach and overwhelmed with empathetic heartache whenever Vanessa and I are together and the conversation and photo-looking turns to her and Johnny. Still, writing *Love Me*—knowing Scott and Jacey are happy—it comforts me just a little.

On a lighter note, probably the most surprising thing to me about the popularity of *Love Me* is the popularity of Carl Harbine! In my secret thoughts, I refer to him as "everybody's favorite secondary character." I've received more e-mails and comments about Harbine than almost any other character in any other book! I'm not quite sure what his appeal is—other than he's just a fun guy and everybody probably knows, or wishes they knew, someone like Harbine. He's just a fun-loving, chubby, sloppy boy who loves Nora more than anything—even Crunch 'n Munch! Yet somehow I was able to pull him out of my brain and onto the page just the way he lives in my mind—to share him with my friends—and I'm thankful for that! He's a feel-good character, and I'm so glad everyone loves him as much as I do.

Oh, just throw my theories on "first love" out the window if you need to! In the end, I simply hope you enjoyed reading *Love Me*. I hope it made you smile and feel youthful—that Harbine pulled a giggle out of you—that Scott Pendleton made you sigh—that you felt Jacey's euphoric joy when Scott asked her if she wanted to marry him in six weeks—and that when you tossed the book onto the pile of books by the side of your bed, you just felt a bit better about your day. So put the CD in or whirl the iPod dial to your "Retro Songs of the '70s" playlist, and emphatically nod your head as you join Donny Osmond in proclaiming to the world that puppy love *is* love! Scott and Jacey proved it.

And now, enjoy the first chapter of
Kiss in the Dark
by Marcia Lynn McClure.

CHAPTER ONE

"Boston!"

Boston skidded to a stop, wishing she were wearing cross-trainers instead of heels. Leaning back, she glanced into Mr. Mercer's office. Dominic Mercer hurriedly rose from his chair, snatching a piece of paper from his desk.

"Yeah?" Boston asked as he strode toward her.

"Are you heading to the set?" he asked.

"No…but I can stop there on my way," she replied. Awkwardly, she rearranged the box, envelopes, and papers piled in her arms.

"Good," Mr. Mercer said, stuffing the paper on top of Boston's already precarious pile. "Then make sure Atkins gets this ASAP! It's an update on that downtown murder."

Boston pressed her chin to the top of the pile to secure the added task. "Got it," she said.

"That's my girl!" Mr. Mercer chuckled, slapping Boston on the behind.

Boston gritted her teeth, nodded, and simply set out anew toward the news desk set. Mr. Mercer was a pervert, and she couldn't stand him! Yet Lara Hoffstetter was leaving the network, meaning the assistant news scriptwriter's job was about to open up. Boston wanted the Channel 7 News assistant scriptwriter's job more than anything. And she was fairly certain she'd get it—as long as she could put up with Mr. Mercer's harassment for a little while longer.

Therefore, she didn't reprimand her lecherous boss, nor would she report him to human resources. She wanted that scriptwriter's job, and she knew she wouldn't get it if she rocked the boat now. Instead, she raced to the news desk, set her pile down just long enough to hand the update on the downtown murder to the media news editor, and hurried on.

Her feet were aching something awful! She'd known she shouldn't have worn new shoes—especially heels—especially on a Friday! Glancing to a wall clock as she rushed down the hall, she breathed a little sigh of renewed determination, knowing she could take her shoes off in just fifteen more minutes. She decided she'd drive home barefoot; she wouldn't wait until she got home to give her feet a break.

"Did you drop that promotional stuff off in advertising for me, Boston?" Ms. Shafer asked as Boston passed an open office door.

"Yes, ma'am, I did," Boston called, not pausing to glance at the woman or give the arrogant promo VP any other opportunity to criticize.

"Fifteen more minutes," Boston mumbled as she tossed a manila envelope onto the desk of one of the weekend anchors.

Fifteen more minutes and she'd be free! Fifteen more minutes and she'd be on her way home to change so she and Steph could go over to Danielle's apartment for dinner.

Boston's mouth watered as she thought of the delicious chili dogs waiting at Danielle's. She could almost smell the onions and cheese, and she smiled. It was always best to have something to look forward to. Boston adored her little secret delights, like knowing a fun evening with friends and chili dogs awaited after a long work week.

"Don't forget the chocolate milk mix," she mumbled. She and Steph were supposed to bring the chocolate milk mix for dinner. Danielle was out.

"Come on, Boston! I need those printouts now!" Mr. Stafford growled as she approached his office.

"I'm sorry, Mr. Stafford," she apologized, handing him the printouts he'd sent her to retrieve. "The printers were out of ink, and I had to change them myself."

"That's no excuse," he growled, snatching the papers from her hand. "I needed these five minutes ago!"

"I'm sorry," Boston said, apologizing once more—though she really felt like slapping him soundly across the face, telling him he should've gone to get his own printouts. She glanced at his potbelly, thinking the walk would've done him good. She kept a civil tongue, however, and turned to drop off the last item she still carried, a box of paper for Samantha Sang's office.

"Thanks, Boston," Samantha said as Boston set the box on her desk and heaved a sigh of relief. "I hope it wasn't too much trouble."

"Not at all," Boston told the head news scriptwriter for Channel 7. "It was on my way," she lied.

Samantha smiled. "I'm sure that's not true…but thank you anyway."

Boston smiled and said, "You're welcome."

Samantha opened the box, lifted out a ream of paper, and proceeded to load her printer. Boston liked Samantha Sang. The woman had retained a good measure of humility, even for her high position on the news staff. She was in her mid-thirties and always dressed well, in business skirt suits. Her overall appearance was very professional and, at the same time, very feminine.

Samantha tucked a strand of short brown hair behind one ear.

"Have you got plans for this evening, Boston?" Samantha inquired.

"Nothing too exciting. Just hanging out with some friends," Boston answered.

"Girl friends…or guy friends?" Samantha asked, winking.

"Girl friends," Boston said, her smile broadening. "We're doing chili dogs and a movie. You know, sloppy clothes, overeating…watching a chick flick."

Samantha giggled. "Sounds like fun!"

"Yeah," Boston said. However, she did not want to overstay her welcome in the office of the woman she hoped to be working for in a few weeks. So she said, "Well, you have a good weekend, Ms. Sang."

"You too, Boston. Eat a chili dog for me, will you?" Samantha said as Boston left her office.

"Of course!" Boston exclaimed.

As she walked down the hallway away from the news scriptwriter's office and back toward the chaos of the news desk set, she crossed her fingers. In truth, she hadn't put in much time at Channel 7 News—only a year—but she'd worked hard, even made some last-minute script changes at Samantha's bidding on occasion. Now she hoped her hard labor, good work ethic, and cheery amity with everyone on the staff would soon pay off.

She felt the buzz in her pocket and retrieved her cell, smiling when she saw the text from Danielle.

Don't forget the chocolate milk mix, it said.

Quickly, Boston responded, *Oh, don't worry…I won't!* speaking the words aloud as her thumbs raced over the keys.

She smiled when Danielle's next text said simply, *Fabulous!*

Boston dropped her phone back into the front pocket of her pants and glanced up at the clock on the wall. Five more minutes—just five more minutes! Yet as her feet ached for relief, she wondered if there would be any feeling left in them at all when she finally got those stupid shoes off.

She raced back to her cubical, quickly straightened her work station, grabbed her purse, and headed for the exit door. As she left, she heard the office go quiet and the Channel 7 theme music begin piping through the building—she knew the 5:30 newscast had begun. Her work week was officially ended!

Boston paused a moment as she stepped from the building and into the warm evening sun. She reached into her purse and dug around until she found one last chocolate Tootsie Pop. She removed the wrapper from the sucker and popped it into her mouth, exhaling a long, relieved sigh of delight. As her mouth began to water from the sweet taste of the candy, she took hold of the white cardboard stick protruding from her mouth and pulled the lollipop out for a moment. She closed her eyes—inhaled a deep breath of city air. All the scents she loved about the city were there: the mingling aromas of the good downtown restaurants, the warm smell of hot pavement, stale pipe smoke wafting from somewhere, a hint of chlorine from the enormous fountain in the plaza one building over.

Boston opened her eyes, popped the chocolate Tootsie Pop back into her mouth, and smiled. She liked working downtown; she wouldn't want to live there but liked working there. As she walked to the parking garage, she passed the Little Christmas Shop. She wished she had time to pop in. She loved wandering through the high-end Christmas decorations, the little lighted porcelain villages. But it would have to wait. Steph would no doubt beat her home and be as impatient as ever to get over to Danielle's.

As she walked, rolling the sucker in her mouth back and forth with her tongue, Boston wondered how Halle's job interview had gone. She wondered if Kara's boyfriend, Max, had managed to get up enough nerve to propose. Surely Kara would've texted if Max had asked her to marry him. Likewise, Halle would've texted if she'd gotten the job. Still, maybe they were just waiting until they were all together at Danielle's for dinner.

Boston slid into the seat of her car, turned the key in the ignition, and backed out of her parking spot. As she drove home, she continued to think about her friends, smiling to herself as she thought of the way they'd all met. The summer after Boston's first year at college, her uncle had secured a job for her at the little Santa's Workshop and North Pole theme park in Cascade, Colorado.

Nestled in the foothills of Pikes Peak, the North Pole had always been Boston's favorite summer vacation destination as a small child. Amid the tall pines and roaming deer, the North Pole had Christmas-themed rides, like a roller coaster that looked like a candy cane, a giant peppermint slide, and a little train that slowly circled the theme park. Santa's house was there, cozy and warm, a fire glowing in the hearth even in summer. There were other little buildings and shops as well—colorful buildings constructed and embellished to mimic a tiny, vibrant alpine village of sorts. Small cafés served hot chocolate, warm cider, cookies, and sandwiches. Deer roamed the park freely, and there was even an area where guests could feed Santa's very own reindeer. All in all, it was the wonder of a small child's dreams come true. Thus, she had been thrilled when her uncle had called with the news he'd procured a summer job for her at the North Pole—for it was just about her favorite place on earth!

Boston stayed with her aunt and uncle in Manitou Springs while she worked that summer. It had been the most delightful job she'd had! Boston smiled as she turned onto Main Street, thinking it still the most delightful job—ever. That glorious summer, she'd started working as the operator for the Candy Cane Coaster but had soon managed to work most days in Carousel Café. It was while serving ice cream and milkshakes at the café that she had first met Halle. Halle worked in the café too—worked in the café or sometimes operated the Christmas Tree ride. Halle and Boston had become fast friends, and they'd soon gotten to know Danielle, who manned the camera at Santa's house. They'd met Dempsey there too, the coolest male elf Santa had ever employed.

Boston giggled out loud as a remembered vision of Dempsey, dressed like one of Santa's elves and operating the world's highest Ferris wheel, flashed through her mind. Dempsey was what Halle liked to call "a character," always into mischief, always finding amusement in the smallest things in life. It was hard to imagine him as the big hotshot he was now—not so hard to imagine that he made his money writing humorous advertising gimmicks and jingles.

Boston, Halle, Danielle, Dempsey, and Dempsey's sister Kara had worked nearly the whole summer together that year before figuring out that Boston's uncle knew all their parents and had procured jobs for each one of them. Thus, the five University of Oklahoma, Oklahoma-born natives found themselves working as Santa's helpers at the North Pole in Colorado for one glorious summer—a summer that forged vastly enduring friendships.

Steph was the only one of the group whom they'd met back at school. She'd worked at small café with Dempsey during their second year. Steph had harbored an insane infatuation with Dempsey and somehow managed to insinuate herself into the group. After graduation, as everyone managed to secure jobs in Oklahoma City, somehow Boston ended up sharing an apartment with Steph. It was a character flaw of Boston's—the inability to say the word *no* when someone acted pitifully enough. Steph had begged Boston to share the apartment, and though her gut churned in telling her she shouldn't cave, she did. Thus, she'd been roommates with Steph for over a year—and in truth, it was wearing.

Boston sighed. Steph was a good girl—and as good a friend as she knew how to be. Yet Boston didn't quite understand why thoughts of Steph caused such anxiety to rise in her. Still, they did, and it seemed the feelings were accelerating. In fact, Boston had been considering getting her own apartment, but she knew that would make Steph angry and hurt.

Scraping the remaining hard candy and Tootsie Roll center off the stick with her front teeth, she deposited the empty stick in the cupholder in the center console of the car—where it would linger for who knew how long with the twenty or thirty other discarded lollipop sticks. Boston shook her head and bit into the now-softened Tootsie Pop. She decided she wouldn't nest on dismal thoughts—not when a fun night at Danielle's was just around the corner. Still, she frowned a moment. It was fun to go to Danielle's nearly every Friday, but secretly Boston wished for something a little more—something a lot more, actually. She dearly loved her friends, but she was beginning to feel stagnant, as if life had begun to pass her by. She hoped then that Max had found the courage to ask Kara to marry him. At least then someone would be stepping into a new adventure—the adventure she secretly yearned to live for herself, the adventure of owning a loving husband and children.

Again she shook her head. She wouldn't think about it. She had a great job—hopefully soon a great career! She would be happy with that, with that and her good friends—Santa's elves or not.

♥

"Do you think I need to have Sylvia put a few more highlights in my hair this time?" Steph asked as Boston pulled into a parking space just in front of Danielle's apartment.

Boston forced a smile and looked to Steph. Green-eyed and brown-haired, Stephanie Crittendon was a pretty girl—at least outwardly. She was tall with a perfectly slender figure and more self-confidence than Boston could ever imagine owning. Yet she was often pretty shallow—very often. Steph had done nothing but talk about her hair all the way to Danielle's. Boston wasn't really just tired of offering reassurance that Steph's hair was perfect; rather, she was more irritated because Steph had answered Boston's cell while she'd been in the bathroom before they'd left the apartment. Logan West had called while Boston had been brushing her teeth, and when Steph had seen the name on Boston's caller ID, she'd taken the liberty of answering instead of just letting the call go to voicemail.

Boston had stepped out of the bathroom just in time to hear Steph flirting with Logan as she promised to give Boston the message he'd called.

"He says he's still at work so he'll call you later…if he gets another chance," Steph had explained. "I didn't want you to miss the call entirely, Boston."

Boston had been inwardly furious! She couldn't count how many times she'd kindly asked Steph not to answer her phone. Further, she knew Steph had answered exactly because it was Logan West. She wouldn't have answered if it had been anybody else.

Logan West was simply the most attractive man Boston had ever known. He'd worked at Channel 7 News until he'd landed a head scriptwriter's job with a competitor. She'd secreted a crush on him simply forever and had been ecstatic when he'd called and asked her out the week before. He'd taken her to the zoo, and they'd had a wonderful time—at least Boston had a wonderful time. Yet she figured Logan had too since he said he'd call again. He had called, and it irked Boston to the tips of her toes that Steph intercepted it. If there was one thing about Steph that she couldn't tolerate (yet still did for the sake of keeping the peace in their apartment), it was Steph's attempts to infiltrate every relationship Boston had. She knew Steph would love nothing more than to steal Logan West's attention—and it was boiling Boston's blood.

Yet as Steph repeated her question, Boston simply bit her tongue, hoping Logan would call back—soon.

"Well? Do I or don't I?" Steph asked.

"I think you have plenty of highlights, Steph," Boston said, forcing a smile. "Maybe you need a few lowlights. Maybe that's what you're thinking is missing."

"Hmm. That could be it," Steph said, pulling down the sun visor, lifting the lighted courtesy mirror flap, and studying herself again. "I'll ask Danielle."

Boston exhaled a heavy sigh. She didn't even know why Steph asked her opinion on anything. She never took it to heart—always had to ask someone else instead.

Boston pulled down the sun visor on the driver's side. She wiped a fleck of dry mascara from underneath one eye—thinking how grateful she was that her own auburn hair held natural gold highlights—closed the mirror, and opened the car door.

"Will you grab the chocolate milk mix, Steph?" she asked.

"Sure," Steph agreed, retrieving the mix from the backseat before getting out of the car herself.

As they started up the sidewalk toward Danielle's house, however, Boston felt her phone buzzing. Quickly she plunged one hand into the depths of her purse, rummaged around a moment, and retrieved the device. She smiled as she looked at the caller ID—Logan West!

"Go on in, Steph," Boston said. "I've gotta get this."

"Okay," Steph said, continuing up the sidewalk while Boston remained still and turned her back to the direction of Danielle's door.

She pushed send, put the phone to her ear, and said, "Hello?"

"Hey, Boston," Logan responded. Boston smiled, delighted by the way his deep voice spoke her name. "This *is* Boston, right?" Logan asked.

"Yep! This time it's really me," she said. Her smile was so broad it hurt. "How are you, Logan?"

"I'm well," he said. "Just wondering if you have time to go out with me tomorrow."

"Of course!" she exclaimed. She worried her excitement was perhaps a little too obvious. "What were you thinking?" she asked, trying to tone down the excitement in her voice.

"Oh, I don't know. Do you golf?" he asked.

"If you can call it that…the way I play," she said. Boston liked golf well enough; she just wasn't very good at it.

"Then we should make a perfect couple out on the course," Logan chuckled. "I stink at it."

She laughed. "Good!"

"I'll get us an early tee-time…like maybe eight a.m. Sound good?"

"Sounds great!" Boston giggled.

"Awesome! I'll pick you up at your place at, say, 7:30?"

"Perfect," Boston said. She smiled at the goose bumps suddenly prickling her arms. Logan West? It was too dreamy!

"Don't worry about clubs. I've got two sets," he said.

"I thought you said you were no good at golf," Boston reminded, mortified that she might have to play with a good golfer.

"I'm not good at all. Just thought it was the clubs' fault the first six months…so I bought another set."

"Did it make a difference in your game?" she asked.

"Not one bit," he chuckled. "See you in the morning then?"

"Of course!"

"Okay. Have a good night."

"You too. I can't wait!" she exclaimed.

"Me neither! Bye, Boston."

"Bye."

Boston sighed with delight, dropped her phone in her purse, and hurried toward Danielle's apartment.

"I cannot believe this!" she exclaimed, giggling to herself. "Logan West! I can't believe it!"

Bursting into Danielle's apartment, Boston began, "You guys will not believe this, but—"

She gasped slightly, startled as Steph stepped directly in front of her and said, "First come, first served. I saw him first. Just remember that, Boston."

"What?" Boston breathed. The determination and warning flame in Steph's eyes confused Boston as much as the threatening tone of her words.

"What the heck, Boston?" Halle asked, rather pushing Steph out of the way and embracing her in a friendly greeting. "What has you all wound up?"

"Just Logan West," she giggled.

"Did he ask you out again?" Kara asked, embracing Boston next.

"He did. We're golfing tomorrow!" Boston said.

"Oooo! That's an all-day event," Danielle said, coming to hug Boston.

"I know! I'm so totally excited!" Boston sighed.

Her friends—they were so important to her. She realized in that moment, consciously realized, how stifling Steph was to her mood—to her very soul. When Boston was in the company of her good friends, she was able to be herself—say and do the things her character and personality naturally did. But when she was sequestered at home with just Steph for company, she was self-conscious, often frustrated, and unhappy. As she gazed into the smiling faces of her true friends, she sighed. Yep, it was time to get an apartment—an apartment of her own.

"Logan West! Mmm! Maybe tomorrow will bring on the first kiss," Halle teased.

"Don't even say that! You know it wigs me out. I get all nervous. The anticipatory anxiety freaks me out!" Boston scolded, smiling.

"But golf is a long game. You have to do *something* while you're walking to the next hole," Danielle said.

"I know!" Boston giggled. She sighed as she thought of Logan's dazzling smile, tawny hair, and broad shoulders. How had she rated a date with him? How had she rated a second date?

"Excuse me."

Boston's smile faded—but only slightly—as a tall, muscular guy pushed his way through her friends and to the door. She recognized him at once from the family photos Danielle had around her apartment—Vance Nathaniel, Danielle's older brother. He was dressed in a pair of swim trunks, a rather ragged white T-shirt, and sandals, and he boasted dark hair, smoldering green eyes, and a rugged five-o'clock–shadowed jaw. Vance Nathaniel was even more handsome in real life than he was in photographs. Boston couldn't help but find her smile suddenly broadening again. Danielle's brother resembled his sister so perfectly—as perfect an example of gorgeous, iconic masculinity as Danielle was the ideal representation of flawless femininity.

"Oh, Vance," Danielle began, "this is Boston."

"Hey," he greeted almost warily it seemed.

"Boston, this is my big, bratty brother, Vance," Danielle said. "And don't let him fool you. Tall, dark, and handsome he may be...but he's a total brat."

"Nice to meet you," Boston greeted.

"You can stay and have dinner with us, Vance," Danielle suggested.

"Yeah! You should totally stay!" Steph exclaimed.

Boston nearly laughed out loud. So Danielle's brother was what Steph had been talking about when she'd nearly growled to Boston, *I saw him first.*

"It's okay," Vance said, shaking his head. "I'm going down to the pool. And besides, nothing messes up a chick party like a ratty, old rooster." He smiled a little, and as Steph sighed with obvious admiration, Boston fought to keep from rolling her eyes with disgust.

"Looks like Steph has chosen her next victim," Halle whispered.

Boston giggled, feeling only sympathy for Danielle's brother. No doubt Steph would pursue him like a rabid pit bull. The guy didn't have a chance.

"You ladies have fun with your chili dogs and girl movies," Vance said. "It was nice to meet you all."

He left the apartment. As soon as Vance had closed the door behind himself, Kara said, "I thought he wasn't coming until next week, Danielle."

Danielle nodded. "He wasn't going to...but his landlord was pressuring him to get out of the apartment so the new renters could move in."

"When will his house be ready?" Halle asked.

"A month, I think. He's just gonna stay with me until it's ready."

"So he's a zookeeper?" Steph asked.

"He'll be the curator of exhibits at the city zoo," Danielle explained. "But he doesn't start for three more months."

"What'll he do until then?" Steph asked.

Boston sighed. It was so obvious that Steph was already planning her wedding to Danielle's brother, wondering how she could time the nuptials just right so she and Vance could move into his house and have a month or two of marital bliss before he started his new curator job.

"He's gonna work road construction," Danielle answered.

"Ooo! That's a brutal job this time of year," Halle exclaimed.

"Yeah…but Vance likes physical work. He likes to keep busy," Danielle said.

"Well, he's gorgeous, I'll give him that!" Steph said.

"I guess so…if you like that kind of thing," Danielle said.

"You mean like rippling muscles, washboard abs, square jaw, handsome face, shoulders like a Viking…" Halle teased.

"Whatever, you guys. He's my brother…so to me he's just the brat who used to drop toads in the tub when I was taking a bath and is way too overprotective of me now," Danielle laughed. "A Viking?" she giggled, looking at Halle. "Maybe a Vulcan?"

Halle frowned. "Like in Star Trek? He doesn't look anything like—"

Steph laughed out loud, shaking her head at Halle's

innocent assumption. "Halle," Steph began, "I swear… you're so stupid sometimes. A Vulcan…like in Roman mythology, not Star Trek. Vulcan was the Roman god of fire and metalwork, and he was ugly. Vance is far from ugly. Sheesh, Halle! Can you at least pretend to have a brain?"

Boston felt sick. She hated when Steph belittled people! She could be so cruel. How had they all put up with her for so long? But the answer was simple: they didn't know what else to do. What could they do, show her the same cruelty she often showed others? Of course not! That kind of cruelty wasn't in any of them—especially Boston. Still, what she'd said to Halle was so unkind.

"Then we'll stick with a Viking," Halle said cheerfully. Boston was ever astonished at the way Halle seemed to let Steph's cruelty just slide away, like water off a duck. "Vance the Viking," Halle giggled. "Can Vikings have dark hair though?"

Everyone laughed. Halle's questions were often so simply—yet so entirely—amusing.

Even Steph laughed, though Boston was certain her roommate was still silently planning her wedding to Danielle's brother, the black-haired Viking.

"So, Boston, tell us about Logan," Kara said then, entirely changing the subject, thankfully. "Are you totally stoked or what?"

"I am," she admitted. "I can't seem to settle down. I mean…I never in a million years thought he'd give me a second thought!"

"Everyone gives you at least a second thought, Boston," Halle giggled. "Those green eyes, that gold-streaked auburn hair, that perfect complexion."

"Whatever," Boston said, rolling her eyes. Halle was always trying to build Boston's self-esteem where her appearance was concerned. "But the question is, did you get the job, Halle?"

"I did!" Halle exclaimed. "I start Monday!"

Everyone squealed congratulations and took turns hugging Halle. Boston glanced to Kara's left hand—no ring on her finger. Max was so in love with Kara—so intimidated by her beauty and self-confidence—and Kara loved Max desperately. She determined she was going to have to give Max a little talking-to—a little more ego boosting. After all, Max already had the ring; he'd shown it to Danielle and Boston only two days before. What the heck was he waiting for?

"Everything's ready for dinner, you guys," Danielle said. "Let's eat…'cause I skipped lunch today!"

At that moment, the apartment door opened, and Vance stepped back in. "I forgot a towel," he mumbled. Boston noted the way he seemed to avoid looking at any one of them directly in the eye. As he strode through the room, her eyes fell to his right leg—to the large, deep scars marring his calf. They literally looked as if something had torn chunks of meat out of him. It was obvious the wounds had been skin grafted. Even though the scars appeared to be very old, the thought of the pain that must've accompanied the injuries that caused them made Boston's stomach flip-flop with sympathy. She wondered what had happened to Danielle's brother to leave such scarring.

Vance disappeared into Danielle's bathroom and returned a moment later with a red towel clutched in one hand.

"Red towels, Danny?" he asked, grinning at her.

"Yeah?" Danielle giggled. "What's wrong with red?"

Vance winked at her and said, "Nothing." Holding the towel with both hands lengthwise out at his side, he stomped one foot and quickly spun the towel around itself, whipping one end out and hitting Danielle on the behind. "Olé!" he chuckled as he left the apartment once more.

"Oh my heck! He's so hot!" Kara giggled. "The girls must be rabid after him, Danny."

Danielle nodded. "Yeah…pretty much," she said, rubbing the cheek of her bum where her brother had whipped her with the towel.

Halle frowned for a moment and seemed lost in thought. "Maybe he'd be a better matador than a Viking," she said.

Everyone giggled and headed for the kitchen area.

"Well, I'm starving," Boston said, picking up a paper plate from the counter. "I skipped lunch today too. I didn't want to be late."

"Me too!" Kara said. "I want extra cheese, by the way."

Boston giggled as she and her friends nearly dove into the buns, boiled hot dogs, slow cooker of chili, and condiments. She loved Friday nights. And she was going to love golfing on Saturday even more!

"Mr. Mercer grabbed my butt again today," Boston said as she sat at the table eating her chili dog.

Danielle put an extra scoop of chocolate milk mix in her glass. "That guy's a jerk," she grumbled. "I don't know how you put up with his behavior, Boston. You should go straight to HR."

"I don't know *why* you put up with it," Steph said.

"Next time he does that, just turn around and drive a knee right in his—" Halle began.

"Oh, don't worry," Boston interrupted. "As soon as I land that assistant scriptwriter's job, I plan to do just that!"

There was a pause as everyone ate in silence for a moment.

"Max and I are helping Dempsey finish his pond thing tomorrow...if any of you want to help," Kara said.

"Well, Boston's going to be making out on the golf course," Halle giggled, "but I can come if you need me. That reminds me—what brand of bra do you wear, Kara? I need to go bra shopping. That's always such a nightmare!"

"Oh, I hate shopping for bras," Danielle whined. "It's torture!"

"It totally is!" Steph added. "I'd rather clean bathrooms than shop for bras."

Boston giggled, enjoying the lighthearted

conversation of her friends. She opened the fridge and took out the gallon of milk, closing the door with her knee. Her eye was drawn to a photograph on Danielle's fridge. A magnet that read, *Eat Beef—The West wasn't won on salad*, secured a picture of Danielle and her brother Vance to the freezing compartment door.

Both Vance and Danielle were smiling, standing in front of a hotel signboard announcing, *Sam Elliott slept here!* Boston gazed at the photo for a moment. Vance's smile was broad—dazzling. Both he and Danielle were much younger in the photo—teenagers—and Boston noted the sparkle in Vance's eyes, a sparkle that had been absent when she'd met him a short time before.

She shook her head, glanced down at her second chili dog, and wondered. Did her mouth water in anticipation of the chili dog on her plate or because a vision of Logan West had just leapt into her mind?

My everlasting admiration, gratitude, and love…
To my husband, Kevin…
Proof that heroes really *do* exist!
I Love You!

ABOUT THE AUTHOR

Marcia Lynn McClure's intoxicating succession of novels, novellas, and e-books—including *The Visions of Ransom Lake*, *A Crimson Frost*, *The Pirate Ruse*, and most recently *The Chimney Sweep Charm*—has established her as one of the most favored and engaging authors of true romance. Her unprecedented forte in weaving captivating stories of western, medieval, regency, and contemporary amour void of brusque intimacy has earned her the title "The Queen of Kissing."

Marcia, who was born in Albuquerque, New Mexico, has spent her life intrigued with people, history, love, and romance. A wife, mother, grandmother, family historian, poet, and author, Marcia Lynn McClure spins her tales of splendor for the sake of offering respite through the beauty, mirth, and delight of a worthwhile and wonderful story.

BIBLIOGRAPHY

Beneath the Honeysuckle Vine
A Better Reason to Fall in Love
Born for Thorton's Sake
The Chimney Sweep Charm
A Crimson Frost
Daydreams
Desert Fire
Divine Deception
Dusty Britches
The Fragrance of her Name
The Haunting of Autumn Lake
The Heavenly Surrender
The Highwayman of Tanglewood
Kiss in the Dark
Kissing Cousins
The Light of the Lovers' Moon
Love Me
The McCall Trilogy
An Old-Fashioned Romance
The Pirate Ruse
The Prairie Prince
The Rogue Knight
Romantic Vignettes-The Anthology of Premiere Novellas
Saphyre Snow
Shackles of Honor
Sudden Storms
Sweet Cherry Ray
Take a Walk With Me
The Tide of the Mermaid Tears
The Time of Aspen Falls